PRAISE FOR A BITCH CALLED HOPE

"A well crafted mystery novel with a heroine you can root for, plenty of action and a satisfying ending."
—PHILLIP MARGOLIN,
New York Times bestselling author of *Capitol Murder*

"A noir with heart. Poker-playing ex-cop Lennox Cooper joins the sorority of lonesome gumshoes. Beware, it's hard to put down."
—CARA BLACK,
bestselling author of the Aimee Leduc mystery novels.

"Gardner deftly balances the detailed intricacy of the police procedural with a richly nuanced tale of betrayed love, family conflict, and murder. Told with a crisp voice and sharp pacing, the story of private investigator Lennox Cooper packs a wallop from the opening scene."
—BILL CAMERON,
award winning author of *County Line*

All In

LILY GARDNER

DIVERSION
BOOKS

Also by Lily Gardner

The Lennox Cooper Book Series
A Bitch Called Hope
Betting Blind

Diversion Books
A Division of Diversion Publishing Corp.
443 Park Avenue South, Suite 1008
New York, New York 10016
www.DiversionBooks.com

For more information, email info@diversionbooks.com

First Diversion Books edition May 2018.
Paperback ISBN: 978-1-63576-381-2
eBook ISBN: 978-1-63576-380-5

LSIDB/1803

To Michael and Mihkel—my deep and abiding love.

CHAPTER 1

Lennox Cooper warmed her fingers around twenty ounces of Starbucks on the way home from her morning walk. She was fiddling with her keys on the porch and didn't look through the windows, didn't see the housebreaker. She let herself in.

Lennox's heart pounded in her ears.

An old woman, seventy if she was a day, had made herself comfortable in Lennox's favorite chair. A home invasion. "Help me," the old woman said. "Please, Ms. Cooper."

Help her what? Hand over her cash box? Quieting her breath, Lennox strained to hear the creak of a floorboard, any sound that signaled a second intruder.

If the woman was carrying, the gun was still tucked in the giant handbag she held on her lap. No way was Lennox going to be held hostage by a little old lady. Lennox launched the twenty ounces of coffee across the living room and sprinted down the hallway to her office.

Lennox heard the woman yell as the cup landed, but

by then she'd reached her desk drawer, where Old Ugly, her service pistol, gave her a fighting chance against the home invaders. Pistol in both hands, Lennox cleared the house from basement to upstairs. The woman had come alone.

When Lennox returned to the living room, the housebreaker was on her knees sopping up spilled coffee with paper towels and a small bottle of spray—something that must've come from her handbag.

"Get cold water before the stain sets," she told Lennox as she dabbed the rug.

Lennox's best rug, paid for by running surveillance on a back-injury disability case. Just about the time she thought she'd die of boredom, this guy who'd been hurt so bad he could never work again drove to a bowling alley. Once Lennox had taken a few pictures of him bowling a spare, the job was over and Lennox collected her money from the insurance company.

And bought her rug. And now spilled coffee all over it.

Lennox reached her hand down. "Get up," she said to the old lady and hauled her to her feet. "I don't know how you got in here, but get out. I'll take care of my own damned rug."

The old woman sucked in her bottom lip, her black eyes enormous behind designer glasses. Whatever game she was playing, she looked like it wasn't going down as she expected. "I've made a mistake," she said. "I should've waited for you on your porch, but I've been so upset."

"That's what you do when you're upset? Break into people's homes? How did you get in?"

She waved a hand at the triviality of the question. "That's not important," she said. "My boy's in trouble. If you don't help him the cops will lock him up for life. I know about you, Ms. Cooper. I read about the sex crime murder last year. You didn't give up even after the prosecutor dropped the case."

The case the old woman was referring to had left a hole in Lennox's heart the size of Greenland. Lennox took a deep breath. "How did you crack my security system?"

"In my business, I get in wherever I need to."

"What business would that be?"

The old lady shrugged. "That's not important."

"Is your son a housebreaker too?"

The woman settled back into the chair by the fireplace. She said her name was Idzi Jagoda. She had gray corkscrew curls, blackbird eyes, a tan left over from the summer. The only thing that would tip a person off that she wasn't a typical grannie was that big old crocodile handbag. Some poor reptile gave its life so the woman would have a place to hold her lock picks.

"My boy, Tomek, calls me at two o'clock this morning. I can't understand him. Finally, I made some sense of it. His girlfriend is dead. Drowned in a hot tub."

"His hot tub?" Lennox said.

"It was out in the suburbs. He'd never been there before. He's crying. Blubbering. The girlfriend had called him. Wanted him to party with her. By the time he got there she was dead."

"Was he sure?"

"Very."

"Who else was there?"

Idzi shook her head. "Just her. Tomek called me right away."

"But not the police."

"He's afraid of the police."

"So what do you want me to do? Look at the body and report it? Get rid of it?"

Idzi seem to turn that idea over in her head. "Could you?"

Lennox stood up. "There's the door. Get your butt out of here."

"Relax. It wouldn't work anyway. What I want you to do is investigate the death. Who knows? It might've been a happy accident."

Lennox's expression wasn't lost on Idzi. The old woman shrugged. "She was the kind of woman that a lot of people would be glad to see go away permanently."

The girlfriend's name was Hadley Eberhart. She had worked at Portland's main library. She was in her early thirties. She and Tomek had been seeing each other at least six months.

Lennox said, "You don't typically see librarians targeted for murder."

"The point is the police would confuse Tomek. Make him say things he doesn't mean."

Idzi made this boy of hers sound dim, so Lennox asked, "Is he slow?" The old woman reddened. Lennox took that as a yes. What a complete and total mess.

"I can't help you," she told Idzi.

"I'll pay you a five-thousand-dollar signing bonus. An extra ten-thousand when you clear my boy."

Lennox didn't answer.

Idzi opened her giant handbag and counted out eight stacks of hundred-dollar bills.

"Signing plus retainer?" Idzi said.

Detectives don't get signing bonuses. Lennox could

rent an office space and quit advertising her home address all over the Internet.

"Look," Idzi said. "I'm a woman used to having my way. So, I bend the law to suit me. You're a detective, maybe you think that I'm not a good person. But my Tomek is good boy. He's an innocent. And he loved the librarian. He'd never hurt her. Never."

"What if I find that Tomek is guilty?"

Idzi wagged her gray curly head. "One thing in this world I know, Tomek had nothing to do with that woman's death."

"The only way I could work for you is if I'm completely free to follow the investigation, wherever it takes me. I'm not going to cover up anything for you or your son."

"Just get him off," Idzi said.

They signed the paperwork. Lennox watched Idzi carefully make her way down the porch steps and into the fog.

First thing to consider was the body. Had the police found her yet? Was the librarian murdered or not? Lennox scrolled through her phone list until she found the Medical Examiner's office. The call went immediately to voicemail. Lennox looked at her watch. It wasn't eight o'clock yet. She scrolled through her phone again and got Samantha King's direct number.

"Hiya. Been a while," Sam said.

Lennox asked about Hadley Eberhart.

"Yeah?" Sam's voice changed from friendly to guarded.

"I wondered if I could take a look," Lennox said.

"She just came in five minutes ago. I haven't even put my gloves on."

"C'mon, Sam. Give a sister a break."

Sam's voice weakened as Lennox knew it would. "Why do you want to see her?"

"It's a hell of a story," Lennox told her. "I'll tell you about it over lunch. My treat."

• • •

The Multnomah County Medical Examiner was a thirty-minute drive from her house. They agreed to meet at one-thirty at a nearby Mexicali Grill, a chain restaurant available only in the outer suburbs.

Sombreros, plastic cacti, and piñatas decorated the peach-colored stucco. Lennox was five minutes late. She started apologizing before she even reached Sam's table. Sam never wore makeup and kept her black hair pulled back in a French twist. She'd picked up some gray since the last time they'd seen one another. The waiter brought them iced tea while Lennox told Sam about Idzi.

"You've got to quit working out of your house," Sam said.

"I know." Lennox opened her notebook and waited.

Sam stared at her for several long moments, then nodded. "I don't have a whole lot yet. Cause of death is drowning. That's for sure."

"Drugs?" Lennox asked.

"You know the tox report takes several days. I can say drinking. Definitely drinking."

"It sounds like this could've been an accident."

Sam shook her head. "Not this time. Bruising on her arms and shoulders consistent with a drowning victim. Even most suicides will fight like holy hell to grab air. But this little gal had yellow latex under her nails. I sent samples to forensics, but I'd say rubber gloves."

"Someone put on rubber gloves to push the vic under water?"

The waiter brought their food. Sam broke off a piece of taco shell and bit it delicately. "That's the way I see it."

"We're talking first degree," Lennox said. "How strong would the perp have to be?"

"I'm guessing Ms. Eberhart was so out of it, breathe on her hard and she would've gone under. And she was little. One hundred twelve pounds."

Lennox tapped her ballpoint on the notes, her lunch growing cold. "Time of death?"

"I'm not ready to say. Could've been around midnight, could've been later. She'd done a refloat. 102 degrees sped up the whole shebang."

Sam elaborated about putrefaction while Lennox tried to eat her enchilada verde.

"Photos?" Sam said.

Lennox pushed her plate away and nodded.

"Look at this one," Sam said. "Even with extensive lividity, do you see the bruising here and here? Now look at the hands."

Lennox could imagine Idzi's boy finding his lover drunk and naked in another man's house and losing it. She took pictures of Sam's photos with her cell phone. Watched Sam finish her lunch.

"What?" Sam said. "You're not hungry?"

Sam scraped her plate clean and shuffled the photos together in a pile. Lennox paid the bill.

"I miss you, girlfriend," Sam said. "These jokers they've

got working Homicide aren't any fun. You should've never let them run you out like they did."

"Spilt milk," Lennox said and shrugged like she didn't care anymore. But she did, she cared a whole hell of a lot.

CHAPTER 2

Lennox called the security guys and told them she needed a better lock system, one that couldn't be opened by an old lady with a good set of files. She spent the rest of the afternoon researching the Jagoda family.

There was nothing damning on Idzi Jagoda, not even a traffic ticket. But Idzi knew how to break into a house and disarm a security system. She carried large sums of cash in her purse. Probably she was one of those wily people that never got caught.

Tomek had an older brother, Pieter, who had done time for possession, intent to sell, and another stint for aggravated assault. Then, three years ago, he'd been arrested for the murder of a female meth addict found beaten to death. The cops released Pieter due to lack of evidence. Pieter was married and had three kids, a mortgage, a car payment, and two credit cards.

Tomek was thirty-one and had finished high school. Back then, so long as a kid showed up for class four years running, the school would graduate him. Ever since high school Tomek had worked at his mother's bakery, except for the sixteen months he spent in prison for possession, intent to sell.

Why would Hadley Eberhart hook up with this man: an ex-felon, a guy who had barely made it through high school? It was time to pay Tomek a visit.

He lived in a small ranch house in a sea of small ranch houses in southeast Portland. A year out of the pen, Tomek had bought the house and paid cash. The house was painted pale blue with white trim. The windows looked newly washed. He kept his grass short and raked free of leaves. Pots of purple and orange pansies crowded his front step.

Lennox patted the cylinder of pepper spray in her jacket pocket before she rang the doorbell. At the very least, the Jagoda family was dodgy. She heard the doorbell buzz over the sound of a television playing in the front room, and waited a moment. No one came to the door, so she rang again, three times. No answer. She rounded the corner of the house to his backyard and came face to face with a hummingbird. Before she could react, the hummingbird zipped away.

Lennox had never seen so many birds in one yard. They chattered and munched on seed. Tomek must've had a dozen bird feeders all heaped with food. Two nuthatches vied for the suet. How many weeks had it been since Lennox filled her lone bird feeder? She pressed her face against Tomek's back window. A large man walked into the kitchen and poured himself a glass of water. He jumped when he saw her face pressed up against the glass. He waved his arm like he was batting an insect. "Go away," he said.

"Your mother hired me," she shouted.

Top to bottom, side to side, Tomek filled the frame

behind the door. He was dressed in a blue tee shirt and camouflage pants. Lennox pressed her PI license against the storm door and told him that his mother hired her to keep him out of jail. He rubbed the stubble on his cheek while he thought it over, Lennox just standing there on his back stoop getting colder.

"So you're a what?" he said. His voice muted through the glass.

"A detective."

"Do I need a detective?"

"Please let me in," she said in a loud voice. "It's freezing out here."

He nodded slowly, unlocked the door, and let her inside. He was so big he could've put Lennox in his pocket, but good-looking for a galoot. He headed back to the living room, threw himself back on the sofa, and stared at the television like he'd forgotten she was there. A football game was being analyzed by two commentators on a sports channel. She sat on the opposite end of the sofa.

Ink covered his crossed arms. His eyes were red and swollen. He looked like he'd spent the morning and most of the afternoon crying. Every few minutes he'd dab under his eyes with a paper towel and blow his nose.

Everything in the living room was painted and upholstered in blue, everything neat as a pin. A copy of *Harry Potter and The Goblet of Fire* lay on the coffee table next to the roll of paper towels. A floor-to-ceiling bookshelf stood against the wall opposite the sofa. Hard-covered Harry Potter books took pride of place.

"You must be a big Harry Potter fan," Lennox said.

"They were a present," he said. "From her." He swallowed hard.

"Is that her?" On the bookshelf under the Harry Potters stood two photos framed in brass, one of them a recent picture of Idzi blowing out birthday candles. The second photo was of Tomek smiling so hard, his eyes were two creases. A woman nestled up against him, a big grin pasted on her face.

"She was very pretty," he said.

"Yes, she was. Your mother hired me because she thinks you might be implicated in Hadley's death."

He chewed on the cuticle of his index finger, his eyes pooling with tears.

"She said Hadley called you last night. At eleven? What did she say?" Lennox said.

"She was all alone. She missed me."

"You couldn't come right away. You were working," Lennox said. "When does your shift end?"

Tomek picked up the remote and jacked up the sound. Everything she didn't want to know about the game shouted from the tube.

The moment he set the remote back on the coffee table Lennox snatched it up and jumped off the sofa. The very last thing she wanted was to wrestle with a large man. She turned the TV off.

Tears ran down his cheeks. "I should've been there," he said. "I could've saved her."

He mopped his face with a paper towel.

"Sometimes being there isn't enough to save them," she told him. And it came back to her, those days after Fulin died. Fulin, the bravest, most beautiful man she'd ever met, her best friend. She and Fulin had made plans. They were going to be partners: Cooper and Chen. And then she blew

18

it. Let hope override her judgment. When he died it had hurt so bad it was hard to sleep, hard even to breathe.

Now she was going to start crying. She told herself to keep it together. "Where was your last delivery?" she said.

"Paul Bunyan on 105th."

She made a note. "Do they sign for deliveries?"

No.

"Okay." Lennox took a deep breath, let it out. "You went to the house Hadley told you about."

He repeated the sequence of events just as Idzi had described it.

"You found her at the bottom of the hot tub," Lennox said.

"She was curled on her side the way she liked to sleep," he said. "She was so beautiful that way, like a mermaid. It was too late." He tore another paper towel off the roll.

It was like Idzi said, how could she not believe this guy? "Just a couple more questions," Lennox said. "Do you know the house that Hadley was partying in?"

No.

"And no one else was with her?"

"She was very pretty," he said.

"Yes," Lennox said. "Was she with anyone else when you got to the house?"

"Just her. At the bottom of the tub."

Heavy fists pounded the door. A rough male voice yelled, "Tomek, let me in."

"My brother," he whispered. He looked anxiously at the door.

"Good," Lennox said, but her heart was beating double time. "I want to talk to him." She kept her hand in her jacket pocket, wrapped around the pepper spray.

Tomek opened the door.

Pieter shoved the heels of his hands against his brother's chest. "Stupid fuck," he said.

He pushed his brother aside and faced Lennox. There was a strong family resemblance between the brothers. Pieter was as tall as Tomek but had a leaner physique. His hair and beard were a lighter blond. He smelled like he'd been sucking on cigarettes since breakfast. "Who are you?" he said.

"I'm the one your mother hired."

"What are you doing talking to him? He can't tell you nothing the old lady hasn't already told you," he said.

"I wanted to hear Tomek's version."

He looked her over from the part in her hair to the toes of her cowboy boots. "Don't waste your time. He's not going to give you any insights."

"Did you know Hadley?"

"A cunt if I ever met one," Pieter said.

Tomek's face turned deep red, but he didn't say a word.

"Where were you from eleven last night until one-thirty?"

"That's the best you can do?" Pieter said. "I get fingered to get my brother off the hook?"

Tomek backed away from his brother until he was up against the bookshelf.

In one fluid move, Pieter reached behind him and pulled out a wicked-looking knife.

He stood nose to nose in front of Tomek, the blade held underneath his brother's chin. "I'll gut the two of you if you try to lay this on me," he said. "And Ma can go to hell."

Tomek's mouth twitched, but he kept his gaze level.

Lennox closed in on the two men until she was reaching distance from them. "No one's trying to say it was you that hurt Hadley," she said in a low voice. Her fingers were wrapped around the pepper spray. A fraction of a second was all it would take for Pieter to cut Tomek's throat.

The brothers stood nose to nose, chest to chest, Pieter's breath heaving like a racehorse. She could see that he'd wanted to kill Tomek for a long time.

Finally, Pieter stepped back and sheathed his knife. "I had nothing to do with your bitch, Dummy. I wouldn't waste my time."

CHAPTER 3

The fog never lifted. Lennox ate a sandwich for dinner, changed her sweater, checked her lipstick, then trudged a mile down the buckled sidewalks along Broadway to the Shanty Bar and Grill. It was Friday poker night with a group of cops and lawyers she'd played with for more than ten years. On a normal Friday, the only thing on Lennox's mind would be how much money she expected to win, but that was before Idzi had made herself at home in Lennox's living room.

Lennox walked under the dripping trees, the vague shapes of dog walkers occasionally moving past her. It was like a dream where she was cold and needed another quilt but was too asleep to get it. She needed to find out more about the Jagodas, and for that she would go to her poker buddy, Fish. Fish worked in Vice and knew nearly every drug dealer and thug in Portland.

Lennox reached the Shanty and closed the door on the fog. The Shanty served generations of folks from Portland's Hollywood district and most of the cops that worked the northeast precinct. The building itself had started out as a flower stall a hundred plus years ago, back when Sandy Boulevard was a single lane dirt road. A hunk of the original flower stall stood as part of the Shanty's back bar. The place was warm, dimly lit, and smelled of fermented malt and fried fish.

One of her poker buddies, 2-K, stood at the bar talking to a young patrolman. 2-K was a tall, skinny guy in his early forties, sandy-haired, freckled and cow-licked. He'd been a patrolman his whole career.

"There you are," he said when he saw Lennox.

"Is Fish here yet?" she said.

No, he hadn't seen Fish come in. 2-K peeled away from the bar and together they marched past the order window outlined in Halloween pumpkin lights to the back room.

The back room where they played poker was paneled in knotty pine from the sixties. A big round poker table with stained green felt stood in the middle of the room beneath a fake Tiffany lamp. The room smelled like spilled beer, old carpet and something more, a smell she couldn't put her finger on, but it was home base for her. Her friend, Ham, sat with his back against the wall stacking two piles of chips. The overhead light caught the silver in Ham's beard and mustache. Had it been that long since college? They weren't even forty yet. Lennox leaned over and hugged him. His lucky shirt was growing ripe. She told him he needed to throw that bad boy in the washing machine.

Not like Jerry, their token attorney, who was dressed in a nice suit.

"You in court today?" Lennox asked him.

Jerry nodded and smiled, his face creasing in a dozen

folds. For all his wrinkles, he was a cutie, a guy who dated women half his age, but a true gentleman.

"There's my pixie girl," he said. "Now the party begins."

"I've had the weirdest day," she told them.

"*You* had a weird day." Fish blew in the door, Sarge right behind him. Fish had the lowest forehead and thickest hair of any humanoid walking the earth since the Neanderthals. He used to be Lennox's enemy, but for the last few years he'd become her go-to guy on the police force.

"I get called out on a 412, domestic violence," Fish said. "It's eleven in the morning. There's blood on the floor, the walls, the table, busted CDs. Reeks of booze. And you should've seen this couple. They're in their fifties, the woman looks like a wart. Her boyfriend's even gnarlier. Anyway, she'd stabbed him a bunch of times."

"Six times," Sarge nodded his bald head.

"They're calling each other names," Fish said. "She says he was playing that fucking stupid Eagles record."

"*Peaceful, Easy Feeling*," Sarge said.

"Over and over. She tells him to stop, for God's sake stop. All night she says. So, she loses it."

Ham restacked the red chips.

"Someone broke into my house," Lennox said.

There was complete silence for a minute.

"Who did you piss off this time?" Fish looked around the table. But no one was laughing.

"Did they hurt you?" Jerry's face was a web of worry lines. "How did you get away?"

"It was an old lady who broke in, sitting in my living room like she belonged there. She wanted me to defend her son on a murder rap."

"Goddamn," Ham said. "How many times have I told

you, get your office out of your house. Your home address is on business cards all over Portland."

"I'll lend you some money if that would help," Sarge said.

"Thanks, Sarge. But I got the money now."

"You took the job," Ham said.

She nodded. Everyone at the table groaned. "I know it sounds crazy, but I met the guy. The old lady's son. He says he didn't kill his girlfriend and I believe him."

"Here we go again." Ham sighed wearily. This was how it was with them since college days: Lennox playing the exasperating little sister to his wise older brother. Which is why she omitted the part about being threatened at knifepoint by Tomek's older brother.

"Are we going to play cards?" 2-K said. "Because if we're not, I'm going to watch *Dancing With the Stars*."

"We'll talk about this later," Ham said.

Ham called the game: five-card stud. Broke the seal and opened a fresh deck.

Lennox's toes curled. What in the wide world was sweeter than the sound of cards clattering against each other in the shuffle.

He dealt the first card down, the next card up. Lovely. She had a pair of twos, the first one hidden.

"Ace high," Ham said. Fish started the betting with two white chips. 2-K, with a jack up, bumped it and threw in three chips. That was one of 2-K's virtues, he was a reckless gambler and a sure income stream for Lennox. Sarge folded.

Ham dealt the next round face up. 2-K was dealt another jack and led the betting. He threw in three chips. Jerry threw in his three. Either Jer had a queen or a king in the hole or he was overly optimistic. Fish folded. Lennox drew a ten of diamonds and should've folded. But she knew in her heart she could beat 2-K.

2-K jittered his leg and started humming *Peaceful, Easy Feeling*

"Shut up," Fish said.

"What?" 2-K looked surprised, like he didn't realize he'd been humming. Ham folded and dealt the next card. Lennox drew the ten of spades. She had two pair, a solid hand. She glanced at 2-K. For all his jittering and singing, he probably had just the pair. Lennox met his three and bumped it another chip. 2-K tossed in another chip.

"You're killing me," Jerry said, but he threw in another chip. It was down to Lennox, Jerry, and 2-K.

Ham dealt the fifth card. Lennox drew a jack. It looked more and more like 2-K was betting on a pair. She stayed in.

'Cause I'm already standing on the ground, 2-K sang under his breath.

"What does that even mean?" Jerry said. "Where else would you be standing?"

"Of all the stupid Eagles songs, it's the stupidest," Lennox said.

"Your bet," Ham said to 2-K.

He threw in four chips. Lennox threw in four.

"*Take it Easy* is dumber," Fish said.

"Enough with the Eagles," Ham said.

"What the hell," Jerry threw in his chips. "Pair of queens."

"Two pair," Lennox said. She started to reach for the pile. Gorgeous, gorgeous chips. This hand would put a good dent in what she'd paid the locksmith.

"Three of a kind," 2-K said. His freckles sparked, his blond hair even whiter in the light from the fake Tiffany lamp. The probability of making three of a kind in five-card was two freaking percent. He hummed the next bar of *Peaceful, Easy Feeling* as he swept the poker chips in front of him.

2-K was short for Sidney Two-Thousand, the amount of money he borrowed from his partner several years ago. 2-K swore he paid his partner back in full, but his partner never confirmed it, kept calling him Sidney Two-Thousand until he retired to Boca Raton. 2-K was left with the name forever.

The whole night went like that. Between 2-K's mindless humming and his brilliant luck, they all were ready to choke him.

They played for three hours, then cashed their chips back into currency. Lennox was down three-hundred bucks. Beefing up her home security had cost her five-hundred. At the rate she was chewing through her signing bonus, she'd be back to scratching by in no time flat. The gang spilled back into the bar. Ham tried to corner her, but she waved him off and caught Fish's sleeve. "Do you know anything about the Jagoda family?"

"That's who hired you? Holy crap!"

"I can't find anything on Idzi Jagoda."

"The Jagodas," Fish said. "You're in over your head." Then his attention veered from Lennox to a woman at the bar. She stood impossibly tall. She was blonde, a Valkyrie. 2-K stopped humming and swallowed. Lennox watched his Adam's apple move down to his shirt collar.

Lennox had heard about her. She was the new girl in town. Her name was Jill Rykoff, the super smart and totally gorgeous prosecutor. Rumor had it that old man Jacobie was grooming her to replace him as DA. Jill stood at the bar, slumming it with three other prosecutors. They made jokes and bought drinks for the cops. Lennox watched Jill reach over and pick up her martini glass from the bar, then tip it to her mouth while every man there watched the graceful line of her throat. The cop she'd been talking to leaned towards her and said something. Jill nodded and made eye contact with Lennox.

"You must be Lennox," Jill said in a loud voice. "Join us."

Lennox waved at the goddess and turned to Fish. "The Jagodas," she said.

But Fish stepped around the tables until he was at the bar, Lennox trailing behind him feeling like a fool. He introduced himself to Jill. "Gregory Bartel," he said. His real name. He praised Jill for that plea deal she made last week.

She thanked him and extended her hand to Lennox.

Jill was one of those natural blondes with dark brows and eyelashes that framed blue-gray eyes. Was it even possible that such a perfect specimen of womanhood wasn't prancing down a catwalk in Milan?

"I've heard so much about you," Jill said.

That could be good. That could be bad.

"The guys I've been talking to say you're a hell of an investigator," Jill continued. "We need more sisters in the business. Can I buy you a drink?"

"Sorry," Lennox said. "I have a thing. Some other time."

She smiled to cover up feeling really crabby. She felt like a garden gnome next to this woman. Lennox tugged on the ends of her hair. She was not used to being the woman not being looked at. She grabbed Fish's sleeve and pulled him away. "Excuse me," she said to Jill.

"What?" Fish said in a peeved voice like he actually thought he was getting somewhere with the Viking goddess.

"The Jagodas," Lennox said.

"They deal drugs. Idzi deals drugs," Fish said. "It's funny money. You could end up with your bank account frozen."

"It's the Hadley Eberhart death. I'm not even sure the cops are calling it murder yet."

"Yeah, it's murder," Fish said. "Someone pulled on a pair of rubber gloves and drowned the woman."

"Have they arrested anyone yet?"

"I'm Vice, not Homicide," Fish said.

"Tell me what you know, and you and me can have a drink with Jill, my treat."

Fish glanced at the bar where Jill was holding court. He heaved a huge sigh and gave it up. The family dealt opiates and cocaine. The old lady had never been convicted of anything. Both her sons made deliveries, but mostly they worked as enforcers. Idzi was the brains of the business.

"I already knew most of this," Lennox said.

"They work out of Marie's Bakery in southeast. Idzi owns the bakery, but good luck. They can smell cop a mile away."

"She knew I was an ex-cop when she hired me," Lennox said. "Anyway, I don't smell like one."

Fish snorted. "The hell you don't."

Her phone rang. It was eleven on a Friday night.

August Kline. He was the first defense attorney to hire her after she'd started her detective agency. Kline was a year older and three inches taller than Lennox, which for a dude was pretty short, but he was cute if you liked proper, tight-assed guys. Lennox did not. She preferred outlaws. Not that that was working out for her. If it wasn't for Kline,

Lennox's business would consist of missing persons and surveillance gigs.

Fish elbowed her in the ribs.

"Give me a minute," she said.

"We've got a new murder case," Kline told her.

"The librarian," she said. "Did they arrest Tomek Jagoda?"

"How did you know?"

"Idzi Jagoda hired me this morning."

There was a long pause on Kline's end. Meanwhile, Fish was having a meltdown.

"That's unusual," Kline said.

"Yeah," Lennox said. "Unusual."

"The preliminary's Monday at 4:30. Can you make it?"

She told him yes and was dragged over to the bar before she could even end the call. Lennox stood next to Jill, her head tipped back to make eye contact with this very tall woman made taller by stiletto heels. She was a freaking female skyscraper.

"Let me buy *you* a drink," Lennox told Jill. "One for you and for one for my good friend, Greg."

Jill's mouth twisted into a wry little smile. "What about your thing?"

"Evaporated," Lennox said, giving Jill the most brilliant high-wattage smile she could muster.

CHAPTER 4

Jeffrey Ito, the man behind the company slogan *Northwest Homes—Paradise is Yours,* owned the house where Hadley Eberhart was found murdered. He was all over the Internet: Facebook, Snapchat, Instasomething. If you were looking for a four-thousand plus square foot house in Lake Oswego or West Linn, he was your go-to guy (or so his ads claimed). His number was plastered all over every site.

He answered the phone on the second ring. Lennox heard the sound of a rolling car in the background.

She identified herself, verified that Hadley had been found dead in his hot tub.

"I need to talk to you today," she told him.

"I don't really understand," he said. "I talked to the police yesterday."

"I'm not working with the police."

"I've already told everything I know to the authorities," he said.

"How about two this afternoon?"

"This is Saturday," he said, in the same way an Orthodox Jew would say *It's the Shabbat.*

"Five, then," she said.

He sighed noisily, like how could she be so clueless. "I have seven showings today. I'll be lucky to finish by eight tonight."

"That will work," she said cheerily. "Where do you want to meet? I guess your house is out."

More sounds of traffic. Lennox waited a couple of moments.

"No. I'm sorry, but I don't think I have to talk to you."

"Where are you staying?" she said. "No. Don't tell me. I'm a detective, I'll find you."

"Not there." He sounded alarmed.

He agreed to meet her at the Heathman at eight. The Heathman was a good choice. The hotel bar was too chi-chi for cops, and all the lawyers she knew congregated at Higgins.

The Heathman pretended to be British. They even had two doormen dressed as Yeoman of the Guard, in red tights and knee britches, a long tunic and ruffled collar. It was hard to say how much the hotel paid these dudes to stand on the sidewalk being smirked at.

Inside it was all marble floors, dark wood, and brass rails. Lennox felt sentimental about the place. She'd been coming to the Heathman for Christmas tea with her mother, Aurora, since she was eleven. Cucumber sandwiches, little cakes, Christmas music playing on the hotel's grand piano. Now Lennox was pushing forty and Aurora, this tiny husk of a woman, smoked on her balcony, stubbing the butts out in an old china teacup. Lennox china, from whence Lennox got her name.

Lennox stepped into the bar. The light was warm and low like a whiskey buzz. She immediately IDed Ito from his social media photo. He sat alone, at a corner table, hunched over a martini. Their waiter came promptly to their table the minute Lennox was seated. He offered her a menu that was bigger than their table. She waved it away and asked for a pot of black tea. Ito ordered another martini.

Ito had been through rehab twice, and judging by the dark circles under his black almond eyes, he looked due for another stay. His hair was cut close around the sides of his head, long and curly on top. He was beautiful in a bad boy way: Lennox's type in a nutshell. She took a deep breath and shook Ito's hand. It was clammy and trembling.

"She was really a nice girl," he said, speaking of Hadley. "The whole thing, her dying at my place, it's really rocked me."

It had to have been a shock, for certain. But if Lennox put herself in Ito's place, would it rock her world to find her ex dead in her hot tub? Depended on the ex. There was one former boyfriend she'd feel a deep satisfaction seeing at the bottom of a pool.

"Tell me about Hadley," she said.

"She loved books. Read all the time. She worked at the main library, that's how good she was, but she had two sides. She had a wild streak, oh my God." Ito drained the last of his martini.

Their waiter placed Lennox's tea and Ito's drink on the table. Picking up the replenished martini right away, Ito took a deep pull from it, then caught Lennox staring.

"Sorry," he said. "I'm not usually like this. I guess it's just talking about her."

"She had a wild streak," Lennox prompted.

"Oh man, unbelievable. We had some good times, but I started missing appointments, having trouble closing a deal. It got bad enough, I thought I was going to lose my house. That's when I went into rehab the second time, got off the coke."

"Is that when you broke up?"

"I tried to help her, get her into NA," Jeff's voice trailed off. "But she wasn't interested."

Hadley remained a constant temptation. So they broke up nine months ago. And then he found Cathy, a girlfriend who helped him be a better man. She got him jogging, wanted the best for him. His business picked up. And he had bonded with her little boy, an eight-year-old named Alex. They'd talked about getting married next year.

"When you broke up with Hadley, did you change your locks?"

Ito nodded.

"But there was no sign of a break-in the night of the murder."

Someone lowered the ambient light in the bar. As it got later, the bar would grow dimmer until it was dark as a cave and everyone would have a buzz. That's what the Yeomen of the Guard were for: *May I call you a taxi, sir?*

"No sign of a break-in?" Lennox said.

There was this one time last summer. Three months ago, maybe. July. Hot. And it had been a bad day. Two deals went south. Hadley had called, said she had some excellent blow. One thing led to another. She might have duplicated the key after he left for work.

There was more. He'd seen her again. And probably again. Lennox could tell by the way he assumed the posture of a naughty, but totally adorable puppy. If she'd had a newspaper, she'd have rolled it up and swatted him.

"You continued to see Hadley even though you had a serious relationship with someone else." She kept her voice flat. No sympathy for puppy-boy.

"Are the police going to hold that against me?" he said. "They suspect the person that calls it in. Am I right? But what could I do? She was in my tub."

Even he knew he wasn't selling it. She said, "So then what?"

"There was a bottle of Stoli on the patio table. Are they going to arrest me?"

"You had a drink," Lennox said.

"What would you do?" He took a long pull from his martini. "I cared about her. She was dead."

"What else did you do?"

Her purse had spilled all over the table and the patio. He hated mess. He just scooped the contents back into her purse.

"What was in there?"

"Stuff you'd expect: Cell, keys, a brush, some makeup."

"No drugs?"

He shook his head, looking guilty as hell. She'd just bet he filched something.

"And they didn't bring you in for questioning?"

"Should they have?" he said.

Why hadn't they taken Jeff in for questioning? He looked like a prime suspect to her. Maybe Idzi was right, the cops never took Ito seriously because they'd already targeted Tomek.

Lennox leaned forward and said, "Did you know that Hadley had a boyfriend other than you?"

"Well." He paused. "I didn't know his name or anything. I think he was a user. She'd say she was meeting someone, you know, but she never said his name. When we'd go out for coffee, she'd get texts."

"Were you jealous?"

"No." He made eye contact the way people do when they want you to believe them. He was lying his face off. She could pressure him, sure, but she let it slide.

"Tell me about Hadley when you came home and found her," Lennox said.

"She was naked. In the tub. Like I said."

"Floating on top? Sunk on the bottom?"

"She was on the bottom, I think," he said. "She could've been floating, maybe just under the surface? I've never seen anybody dead before. I must've gone into shock, I'm not really sure."

"You've never seen anyone dead before, but how did you know she was really dead?"

"I just knew. You can't float face down for that long."

"And you didn't try to save her?"

A bit of spittle formed at the corner of Jeff's mouth. He wiped it away with his finger.

"What time did you find her?" Lennox said.

Jeff had spent the night at Cathy's, left her house a little before seven in the morning for a change of clothes.

"When did you show up at Cathy's?"

He'd had a late showing, arrived at Cathy's house just before nine. The kid was already asleep. Cathy heated up some dinner for them. They watched TV. Then Jeff got a call from Hadley. She was high and wanted to party. She wanted to borrow money.

"I had 30 seconds to get off the phone, or I'd be hearing about it half the night."

"Cathy sounds protective."

"Oh yeah." Ito looked down at his hands. They were clasped tightly together. He wasn't impressing Lennox with his commitment to the straight life with Cathy and child.

"Did Cathy ever meet Hadley?"

Ito shuddered. "You think I'm nuts?"

But how could he know for sure? Hadley worked at the public library. What could be easier? "So you had 30 seconds to get off the phone with Hadley," Lennox said. "What did you say?"

"I told her no. Absolutely not. She told me to go fuck myself." Ito shrugged. "Sorry for the language."

"Did Hadley tell you where she was?"

No.

"But isn't that a little odd?" Lennox said. "She wants you to party with her, but doesn't tell you where she is?"

"If I knew she was at my house, I would've gone there, kicked her out."

Maybe that's exactly what he did.

"I need Cathy's last name and her phone number," Lennox said.

"Please don't bother her," Ito said. "The police have already talked to her. She's very upset."

"I can wait." Lennox shrugged. "But then I have no incentive to keep your secrets."

Her name was Cathy Dunlap. Ito gave Lennox her phone number.

What was he scared of exactly? That Cathy might leave him? Or was it deeper than that? She was his alibi. How iron-clad was that alibi?

CHAPTER 5

August Kline drew the 4:30 slot with Judge Eleanor Martinez presiding and Jill Rykoff as the prosecutor in the case of the State of Oregon versus Tomek Jagoda. Lennox sat behind the bar in the row designated for the defense attorney's staff. She watched the guard lead Tomek into the courtroom. He was dressed in a dark suit, but no tie. The suit jacket strained across his shoulders and the trousers were tight in the thighs. Lennox wondered if he'd borrowed the clothes from his older brother.

For a big man in an ill-fitting suit, Tomek moved with ease. His body was graceful, but his face was numb. A jail face. This wasn't the first time Tomek had been incarcerated. He took the seat next to Kline just before the bailiff announced the entrance of Judge Martinez. They all stood.

After the judge was seated, Jill Rykoff remained standing behind the counsel table. "We are presenting evidence to Your Honor for moving forward with the charge of first-degree murder against Tomek Jagoda in the murder of Hadley Eberhart. We have evidence that links

Tomek Jagoda to the victim. Evidence that directly ties him to the scene. Evidence of joint involvement between the victim and Tomek Jagoda in illegal activities."

Jill was dressed in a pencil skirt and a pale blue blouse that draped the way clothes drape on super models. What was this woman doing working the crime scene in Portland when she could be speeding down the Grand Canal in Venice on her way to her fabulous palace? Or in New York, Rome…somewhere where the other super-humans walked around.

Kline would normally be jotting notes and sifting through papers at this part of the hearing, but he had turned towards the prosecutor, his ears very pink. And sure, Lennox was sitting behind him and all, but she could tell a whole lot about Kline's state of mind from the color of his ears.

"How do you plead?" the judge asked Tomek.

Tomek pulled himself out of his chair. "Not guilty." Said in a low voice so soft, Lennox could barely make it out.

The judge banged her gavel. "So entered." She leaned forward from the bench. "Because the defendant is charged with a capital crime, no bail is set."

Lennox knew that Martinez wouldn't consider the bail, but somewhere in her heart she had hoped for it.

Chairs scraped across the stone floor and everyone stood as the judge exited the courtroom. A guard marched over to the defense table. Tomek shifted his feet and pivoted to catch Lennox's eye. He cast her a pleading look, as if she alone could save him. The guard led him away.

Jill walked over to the defense table and shook hands with Kline. She turned and gave Lennox a ghost of a wink. More of that sisters-in-criminal-justice thing, Lennox figured.

"Do you have a moment?" Jill asked Kline. He nodded, his ears even pinker than before.

Lennox leaned over the bar and poked him in the back with her pen.

"What?" he said irritably.

"Do we have a meeting tomorrow?"

"I'll have discovery to you by one o'clock tomorrow," Jill said to Kline.

Kline pulled his phone from his pocket. "Nine," he said to Lennox, then turned his attention back to Jill.

"Tomorrow night?" Lennox said.

He nodded his head without even turning back to her. She could have been a paperclip on the table once Jill started talking to him. The two attorneys traded compliments and bullshit. Lennox left the courtroom. They didn't notice. Kline's ears never pinked when he talked to Lennox. Why the hell did she even care? It was not like she was harboring any secret desire for August Kline. But it felt bad and she didn't know why, and she was a person who wanted to know everything: every secret, every motive. She'd made a career of it.

• • •

A patrolman pushed past Lennox as she descended the courthouse steps. She perched on the brink of cussing him out before he apologized. "Sorry," he said. "I'm late for a poker game. I didn't mean to run you down."

He was cute as hell. Fortyish, auburn-haired, and

freckled. Tall and lanky, the way she liked her men. And a poker player. Well, well.

"I never want to get between a man and his poker," she said.

He grinned. He had great teeth. "Shawn Boyle."

"Lennox Cooper."

"Oh." He got this complicated look. She'd seen that look before from cops. It came along with a rude comment. And whatever they said was probably true.

Back when her partner died, the police board charged her with immoral conduct and failure to follow procedure. If she'd been a man, she would've gotten a reprimand, but she was a woman having an affair with a fellow cop. So when she found her lover shot and bleeding out, she ran and pulled him to cover. Lennox saved his life. Her partner drew fire to save hers and was killed. Back then Lennox hated herself enough that she never stood up for her own interests, never contested the board's ruling. She knew that some of the guys in the police bureau still talked about her.

"Right," she said. She didn't wait for him to reply. Spine straight, she marched down the rest of the stairs and headed to her truck.

"Wait a minute," she heard from behind her. She kept marching.

It started to rain. Shawn trotted past her, then turned so that he faced her. She kept walking, so he jogged backwards. His face flushed with running.

"What do you want?" she said. Cranky, but still willing to concede that maybe she'd misjudged him.

He almost ran over an old guy who shouted at him, "Watch where you're going!"

"Stop before I hurt someone," Shawn said.

"What?" she said. But she could feel herself grinning.

"How about a cup of coffee?" he said.

"I thought you had a poker game."

"Less time to lose my shirt," he said.

"I play poker."

He fell in step with her. "How about a beer instead?" he said. "And a snack. Are you hungry?"

She always was a sucker for charm.

CHAPTER 6

Lennox decided it would be easier and cleaner to refund Idzi's money. She retrieved Idzi's retainer and the signing bonus from her safe, subtracted out her expenses, and charged the old woman for her locks and the security upgrade as well. After the money she lost at poker, Lennox was only a couple hundred bucks to the good.

She stuffed all that luscious cash into an envelope and drove through the rain across the Hawthorne Bridge into southeast Portland, her thoughts a confusion. There was the bonus and all the things she could've done with it. And there was Shawn. How lovely it was to have a beer with a handsome patrolman, a guy that got her in a specific way. A cop way. Oh, but the money…she could've put a first, last and security on an office, and who would know? But if Kline found out, she could just imagine his face, tight-lipped and pissy, thinking Lennox had taken a bribe. And what about Kline? Sure as sure, there was chemistry between him and the prosecutor.

Lennox parked the Bronco on the curb across the street from Marie's Bakery, the Jagoda stronghold.

The bakery was a one-story, flat-roofed building near the bridge on Clinton Street, in a neighborhood that was considered unfussy. Which was to say not gentrified. Not yet.

An old-fashioned bell attached to the door rang when she entered. The smell of yeast bread and sugar eddied around her. There was ancient linoleum and large windows curtained in red and white checks. The women behind the counter, the customers in line, the mothers and their children seated at the tables, even the old man hunched over a mug of coffee turned and stared as she walked in. The room quieted. Suspicion rose off the clientele like the smell of burnt coffee. Okay, so she wasn't Polish. And she still entered a room like a cop. Fish had warned her about that.

Lennox spotted Idzi in tears sitting at a table with three other old women. Idzi dabbed her eyes with a handkerchief. When she spotted Lennox, she stood up and murmured something to her friends. They turned in their seats, scowling at Lennox. She'd just bet that she'd been blamed for Tomek's arrest.

"Follow me," Idzi said. She lifted the end of the counter and motioned Lennox through. Lennox patted the canister of pepper spray in the back pocket of her jeans. They went through the kitchen, past shelves loaded with white plastic bins and stainless steel bowls. Pieter Jagoda appeared alongside a rack of baked goods and fell in step, walking closely behind her. Too close. The baker and the dishwasher looked up from their work, then immediately looked down.

Idzi took a right, and they walked down a narrow hall

to a windowless office. The room was crowded with boxes of foodstuffs stacked right to the ceiling. A chair and an old wooden desk stacked with invoices and banded-together order books were the only pieces of furniture.

"Close the door," Idzi told Pieter. The three of them stood in the cramped space between the chair and the stacked boxes. Pieter stood up against Lennox. He touched her hair. She smelled the sharp tang of his deodorant over the smell of unwashed clothing and smoke. He was trying to scare her, she knew that, but she couldn't make her body not react. His cigarette breath rasped behind her.

"Why didn't you call me immediately when Tomek was charged?" Idzi said to Lennox.

"That's your attorney's responsibility." Lennox kept her voice even and strong. She'd be damned if she'd let these people intimidate her. "Mr. Kline had a meeting with the prosecutor. He might have more for you."

Lennox and Idzi stood face to face in the cramped office, Idzi pissed off and tear-stained. A dangerous combination. Lennox felt Pieter behind her, lifting her jacket, tracing the can of pepper spray she'd stuck in her back pocket. Lennox stepped back and stomped on his boot with her heel, then pushed right into the supply boxes to gain some space. The stack of boxes tipped, but held steady. Now she could see him, unshaven and angry.

He grabbed her by the arm. "Do that again, I'll hurt you."

"Stop it, Pieter," Idzi said then turned to Lennox. "I paid you to keep my son out of jail."

"No." Lennox used her reasonable voice with enough edge to let Idzi know she wasn't going to be pushed around. "You paid me to investigate the librarian's murder and I'm doing that. I've interviewed Tomek, the medical examiner, and the man who owns the property where Hadley was murdered."

"Why wasn't that man arrested? It was his house."

"I wonder that, too," Lennox said. "He is a suspect."

Idzi shifted from foot to foot. "Pieter will make him talk."

"You're not so stupid as to sic Pieter on a witness," Lennox said.

Idzi blew her nose. "I knew this would end badly."

"What do you mean 'end?'" Lennox said.

Idzi waved her hands helplessly.

"I met Tomek," Lennox said. "I believe he's innocent, and I'll work my ass off to get him released." Lennox reached in her bag and both Idzi and Pieter lurched towards her. Lennox pulled out the thick envelope of money. She had to force herself to hand it back to the old lady.

Idzi looked confused. "What's this?" she said.

"It's the balance of your retainer plus the bonus," Lennox said. "I work for Kline on defense cases. He'll include my services when he bills you."

Pieter made a grab for the envelope, but Idzi pulled it close to her chest.

"How come you never paid for a detective when I got arrested?" he said.

Lennox had seen that look before, when a man disrespected or unloved grows angry and violent.

Idzi waved a dismissive hand in Pieter's direction. "You can't get out of this," she said to Lennox. "You're responsible for my boy's fate."

"I've been picked up before," Pieter said. "Did you cry for me too, old woman?"

Did Idzi order Pieter to drive to Jeff Ito's place and kill Hadley? He was absolutely capable of it. While they were having their mother and son moment, Lennox pushed past Pieter and ran out of the room, past the baker and the dishwasher, and under the counter. The old-fashioned bell tinkled as she slammed out the door.

She got to her truck and gunned the motor. The pisser was she could've kept the money. Neither Pieter nor Idzi gave a goddamn about the money. It was all about who loved who and how much.

Lennox was never going to get her off-site office, but she'd kept her self-respect, goddamn it.

CHAPTER 7

Hadley's neighborhood ran along the bottom of a creek bed known as Tanner Creek. Over a hundred years ago, the residents let their geese graze the ravine and the place earned the nickname Goose Hollow. Then developers came in, buried Tanner Creek under fifty feet of dirt, and built Canyon Road. The Vista Bridge, instead of reaching across the creek, now spanned two lanes of traffic. The bridge had been a favorite jumping off place for suicides until the city built a twelve-foot fence on both sides of the bridge. The geese that used to freely roam the neighborhood were long gone.

Lennox circled the area and eventually found a parking spot three blocks from Hadley's place. She marched in the rain past a young homeless woman pushing a shopping cart heaped with stuff under black plastic. The woman was arguing with herself, and when Lennox tried to hand her money, the woman screamed, "Get away from me!"

Lennox kept walking until she reached the slate courtyard that fronted the Winston Apartments, a grand old four-story brick building. Extravagant tile work ran along the foyer and hallways.

Hadley's apartment was halfway down the hall on the second floor. Idzi Jagoda wasn't the only one who could pick a lock. Lennox let herself in. The place was smaller than her mother's walk-in closet. It smelled like old books and candle wax.

What else? What was here that the cops could've missed? Lennox opened the blinds and turned on the lights. A film of fingerprint powder coated the few pieces of furniture and all the window sills and counters. Hadley's queen bed had been stripped of linen. Lennox wondered if the cops had identified who Hadley had been having sex with.

Stacks of books, some from the library, lined the walls under the windows. Most of them were reference books on learning differences. She riffled through every single one of them. Strips of paper marked sections Hadley had been interested in. Hadley had underlined certain paragraphs, occasionally wrote notes in the margins. Tomek's house was full of books, some of them gifts from Hadley. Had she taught him to read?

Lennox found vodka in the freezer; wine, lettuce and peanut butter in the refrigerator; cereal in the cereal boxes. She checked the cupboards, the floorboards, the baseboards. Felt under the window sills, the trim around the doors, the legs of all the furniture. She examined Hadley's clothes, went through all her pockets. The faint smell of jasmine perfume hung in the air.

Lennox pulled a kitchen chair over to the closet and searched the shelf above Hadley's hanging clothes. Two cardboard boxes of printer paper stood stacked alongside a straw hat. Lennox carried the boxes to the kitchen table. Underneath a couple sheets of blank paper was a manuscript—case studies about working with illiterate adults to help them learn to read. Hadley cited various experts in the field and their strategies, but it looked like the case studies were her own. So, the party girl was writing a serious book. *Saint Hadley*. Not just a party bimbo, not just a saint.

Jeff Ito, Lennox could understand. Good looking, good with women, good at selling houses. Long hours, messed-up weekends showing houses day and night. Easy to imagine him drinking the third martini, snorting a line of coke, then morphing from a decent guy into an addict.

But Hadley, what was her story? How did she go from the world of books to drinking and drugging? She worked regular hours, had a noble purpose—what happened? Lennox made a note to check Hadley's parents, siblings, and childhood friends.

In the drawer of the nightstand, Lennox found a plastic wheel of birth control pills along with a half dozen foil packets of Trojans, a roll of antacid, and some paper clips.

Who spent time in this apartment other than Hadley? A lover or lovers. Friends? Lennox canvassed Hadley's neighbors.

An old man on the first floor answered her knock. He lived directly under Hadley. His rheumy eyes checked out Lennox head to toe, then he invited her in. His apartment was overheated and smelled like unwashed clothes. His name was John Holt. He'd lived in the Winston since 1977. He insisted that Lennox sit on his gnarly sofa. A knit afghan in zig-zags of orange, tan, and dark green draped over the sofa back. Once she sat down, he plopped down beside her, coming damn close to touching her. She scooted to the end of the sofa and then reassured him that everything was fine, he wasn't a dirty old man, the thought never occurred to her. She asked him about Hadley Eberhart.

Yeah, he remembered her. A cute little chickie. Party girl. He didn't have a problem with that, hell he grew up in the sixties. She used to make quite the ruckus. Playing records, screaming at her boyfriend, having noisy sex. Holt grinned. The man was a serious creep. Hadley had quieted the last six months, Holt told Lennox. This new boyfriend maybe was a good influence. Not that Holt hadn't seen the old boyfriend around, standing in the courtyard, smoking, waiting for Hadley to come home and let him in.

"What did the old boyfriend look like?"

"Tall. Skinny. Asian."

Lennox showed him a photo array of six Asian men she'd prepared the night before. He studied the pictures and identified Jeff. She had him initial the photo and sign the back. Then she showed him a photo array of six fair-haired men.

"Maybe this guy," he pointed to Tomek. "I can't really say."

"Take your time," Lennox said.

Holt glanced at the faux wood wall clock on the living room wall. "My show is gonna start now." He reached across Lennox for the remote control, but how was Lennox supposed to know that? She jumped to her feet. He blithely turned his television on and changed the stations, apparently not realizing how close he came to getting the shit knocked out of him.

A guy like him had no boundaries. "One last question, Mr. Holt. Were you and Hadley friends?"

Holt seemed hypnotized by the talk show he was watching.

"Mr. Holt?"

"She looked right through me," he said, his eyes never leaving the TV screen. "You get to be a certain age, you're invisible."

Lennox finished canvassing the building, noting the apartments she'd have to come back to in the evening. Then she headed to Hadley's workplace.

The Multnomah County Central Library was more than one hundred years old. The Georgian Revival brick and stone building anchored Taylor and Tenth, taking up a full acre of the city. The library was a beautiful temple to readers and a meeting place and restroom for the downtown homeless.

Armed with photographs of Idzi, Tomek, Pieter and Jeff, Lennox started with the librarians. Hadley's old boss told Lennox that Hadley was irreplaceable, then launched into twenty minutes detailing Hadley's reading program and the number of hours Hadley booked as a volunteer.

"She was a drinker," a chubby co-worker told Lennox. Another co-worker described her as a loner. "Always cheerful," another said. The staff, with the exception of the chubby woman, seemed to like Hadley, but no one knew her outside of work. She never lunched or shopped with any of them. None of them found that odd. "She was a book person."

So, Lennox took it outside.

What Lennox knew from the days when she was a cop was that the homeless favor a particular neighborhood and know their neighbors better than Lennox knew hers. She went from person to person showing them photos of the Jagoda family. About the time she was ready to call the afternoon a bust, a particularly filthy old dude recognized Idzi Jagoda.

"Oh, yeah, she's been in there," he motioned with his gray head in the direction of the library. "I've seen her four, maybe five times. Once I saw her with that little girl. The librarian girl. You know, that kid liked to get high." He nodded. "I could smell it on her, see it in her eyes."

Good God, a lead. Lennox fished a photo of Hadley from her shoulder bag. "This library girl?"

"Yep, she's the one. Saw her with the old one." He pointed a dirty finger at the photo of Idzi.

Lennox asked if she could take down his name as a witness. John McDonald, he told her. Didn't have an address, but she could always find him here at the library. Lennox thanked him and shook his dirty hand.

"President William Howard Taft was here yesterday," he told her. "Now there's a man who likes his food."

CHAPTER 8

The sweet fermented smell of sauerbraten from the Rheinlander seven blocks away seeped in through the front door as Lennox unloaded five banker boxes full of discovery and stacked them in the corner of her dining room.

Jill Rykoff must've flogged the investigators to gather so much information in so short a time. And now Kline expected Lennox to sort, digest and come up with a strategy in six and a half hours for their meeting that night. She made a pot of black tea and began the long task of sorting, reading, and making notes on the crime scene analysis.

• • •

Lennox met Kline in the lobby of his office building at nine. Lit windows from the neighboring offices were faint and smudged in the fog. Kline's coat was unbuttoned, his tie was missing, and his trousers were wrinkled. His chin and jaw were dark with stubble. She liked this rumpled look on him.

"What happened?" she said. "You run out of scotch?"

"Feel like a martini," he said. "And I could use the walk."

They trudged through the cold fog to Higgins, both lugging their briefcases. Lennox's was weighted down with her notes and crime scene and autopsy photographs.

Kline held the door for her, and they headed for the corner booth where they both had a view of the door, making sure they were out of earshot from the other patrons. The bar was warm, the light dim and yellow. The whole place smelled of good cooking. Lennox wished she'd taken the time to eat dinner. Kline ordered the drinks.

She showed him dozens of photos of the crime scene: the hot tub, Hadley floating in the hot tub, the landscape bordering the hot tub, the back of Jeff Ito's house, his open slider. The chemical analysis of the water in Jeff's hot tub. Endless autopsy photographs of the bruises around Hadley's shoulders, chest, and neck. The autopsy report indicated that she had damage to her rotator cuff, presumably from resisting her murderer. Shreds of latex under her fingernails were consistent with a pair of heavy rubber gloves. The waiter who brought their drinks glanced down at a particularly grisly autopsy photo and splashed part of Kline's martini on his cocktail napkin. Lennox pulled the photos out of harm's way.

"A preliminary test for drugs and alcohol came back from the medical examiner. Hadley would've blown a .118 blood alcohol count if she could've blown. Now for the bad news," she said. "They found a pair of damaged rubber gloves, size extra-large, in a dumpster two blocks from Tomek's house."

"Shit," Kline said under his breath.

"They have to be a plant," she said. "He's not that stupid."

Kline looked unconvinced. "Where are the gloves?"

"They're still at the lab."

Lennox told him she hadn't found anything of particular interest in the bajillion interviews the cops had conducted with Jeff's neighbors, Hadley's neighbors and co-workers, Hadley's family (dead parents, no siblings), friends (no one close), or the customers that frequented the bar she went to.

"But here's the deal," Lennox said. "The lead investigator is a guy named Richard Sloane. Dick the dick. I've seen his work. He ran the investigation when Fulin was killed. Didn't believe a word I said until a Seattle cop proved that I was right. I've just started canvassing and I came up with two interesting bits. Hadley's downstairs neighbor saw Ito hanging around Hadley's courtyard even after she was with Tomek. And a guy from the library saw Idzi with Hadley." Lennox didn't feel the need to mention that her witness had also seen a president who'd been dead for almost 90 years.

"Nothing wrong with going to the library." Kline ran his thumb up the side of his martini glass. "Maybe Idzi likes books. What else?"

She told Kline about the inventory of everything in Hadley's apartment: her stacks of mail, a year's worth of phone records.

"The phone records show Tomek's relationship with Hadley six months prior to her death," Lennox said. "There were lots of calls to Jeff Ito and just as many to a number that turned out to be Doctor Jim Slocum. The night of her murder she'd made two calls to Tomek, a call to Jeff Ito, a call to Dr. Slocum's personal phone, and a call to a Terry Purcell, a guy that doesn't exist according to the cops."

Kline drained his martini and squared his shoulders. "Okay, they have the gloves that may or may not be a plant. Jagoda was Hadley's boyfriend. What else?"

"They found a silver foil packet with traces of cocaine and high-grade heroin in the rhododendrons by the hot tub. It had Tomek's distinct thumbprint."

Their waiter showed up with another round. Lennox had barely touched her first one.

"Your thoughts?" Kline said.

"The fingerprint could be a plant as well," she said. "Jeff Ito's a mess. I've interviewed him already, and he changed his story a couple of times. If we assume he wanted to hang onto Cathy, then Hadley becomes a liability." Lennox turned to the pages in her notebook where she had Jeff Ito's interview. "So here's a scenario: the victim calls Ito the night of. She's abusive when he won't lend her money or drugs. He waits for Cathy to fall asleep then drives to his house. Finds Hadley drunk and drugged. Pulls on a pair of gloves and drowns her. Drives over to Tomek's and dumps off the gloves in the dumpster."

"Does Ito know Jagoda?"

"Not that he'll admit yet. But like I said, the guy changes his story every couple of minutes." She took a long pull off her drink. It was late and she was dog tired from all the reading. She didn't know how lawyers managed it. She told Kline about Cathy, Jeff's girlfriend. Ito made her sound like a jealous woman. They both had a motive and they both provided each other with an alibi.

"Then there's Dr. Slocum, Hadley's prescribing doctor," she said. "Who has their doctor's personal phone number?"

"Not me," Kline said. He was starting to relax. Maybe

it was the list of credible suspects she'd pulled together so far, or maybe it was the martinis.

"He prescribed opiates for the victim. But with the HIPAA laws, it's useless trying to get any refill records."

"You mean even you can't wiggle your way around HIPAA?" Kline smiled a crooked smile, the one he used exclusively when he was being ironic. She adored that look. She watched him over the top of her drink and paused for a moment in the warm haze that was the Higgins bar.

"What I wonder about is the Jagodas," she told him. "Nothing about either Pieter or Idzi in Rykoff's discovery."

"Why the hell are you looking at them?"

"Don't you get it?" she said. "Why weren't either Idzi or Pieter even mentioned? Wouldn't Dick the dick have something about investigating them?"

The front door opened and Jill Rykoff clattered across the marble floor in stiletto heels with two prosecutors in tow. Her platinum hair brushed her shoulders. She was fucking luminous. And obviously high.

"Will you check with Jill, make sure we got everything?"

"Sure," he said.

"The toxicology report isn't in yet," Lennox said. "But the medical examiner said what with the victim's blood alcohol count, she could've drowned anyway."

Kline had left off listening to Lennox and was staring at the vision that was Jill.

Lennox kicked his shoe. "Are you listening to me?" she said.

"We've got six weeks until the trial. Let's meet in two days. I'll have Kimberly call you with a time."

They both watched Jill perch on the edge of the bar stool, one very long leg extended, her skirt strained tightly along a slender thigh. Lennox was starting to seriously dislike this woman.

"I've got an interview with Jeff's girlfriend tomorrow," Lennox said.

"Hmmm."

"And I'll set up an appointment to see Dr. Slocum."

She sipped her drink and watched Kline watch Jill.

"Idzi and Pieter," Lennox said. "I definitely could see either one of them drowning the victim."

"You have a cop friend in Vice. Talk to him."

Jill glanced over at their booth and waved. She had a friendly little grin on her face. It took some effort, but Lennox managed to smile and wave back. She looked across the booth at Kline. His ears were red hot.

"Is it just me or are we having more fog this year than normal?" she said.

Kline signaled the waiter for another round. Lennox hadn't finished her first one.

She told him goodnight.

CHAPTER 9

Very few people cooperate with a private investigator out of their sense of fairness and decency, so Lennox had to resort to the biggest tool in her toolbox: guile. "Jeff is the defense's number one suspect," Lennox told his girlfriend, Cathy. "If you want to see him cleared, you'll cooperate with us." That got her attention.

Lennox met Cathy Dunlap in front of the Big Pink, a steel and glass skyscraper that looked like a tall pink bar chart. Cathy stood five foot nine, sleek in Lycra leggings revealing lean muscled legs and a tight little tush, the kind of body that took two hours a day of hard training to achieve. Cathy had worked as a mortgage underwriter for seventeen years. Good credit, no priors. She'd been married for ten years, divorced for five. Her son was eight years old. She was forty-seven, fourteen years older than Jeff.

Cathy asked to see Lennox's license, then studied it forever. It started to rain.

They ran north along Pine Street for five blocks. Cathy ran with the kind of light floating step that made non-runners want to take up running. And fast. Lennox pounded the sidewalk with every step. She followed Cathy as she headed for the river promenade that stretched from the Steel to the Hawthorne Bridges, the two-mile-long Waterfront Park.

It wasn't as if Lennox wasn't a good runner. She trained five days a week, but Cathy was sprinting. All Lennox could do was keep up with her. She was going to come out of this thing with no more knowledge than she already had.

"Stop," Lennox said in a loud voice. Cathy was already ten feet ahead. "We need to sit down and talk."

Cathy turned around and smirked, a micro smirk, like she'd proved something. Lennox wanted to hate her, but that wasn't going to get her anywhere.

"Let's get some lunch," Lennox said.

"I don't eat lunch," Cathy said.

"Of course you don't. You want to sit on a bench in the rain."

Cathy grudgingly agreed to go to Mother's Bistro, a couple of blocks away.

You'd think that two soaking wet women in Lycra workout clothes would not be seated in a nice restaurant. You don't know Portland.

"This way," the host said and ushered them to a table.

Mother's Bistro served up comfort food like your mother made if your mother was straight out of the Nickelodeon fifties. Crystal chandeliers hung from Mother's very high ceiling. Even so, it was more comfy cozy than elegant. And the place was crowded. It was always crowded.

Lennox shivered as she slipped off her backpack, certain that she'd leave a wet imprint of her butt and the back of her legs on the chair's upholstery. She fished out her notebook and a pen.

They both ordered hot tea. Lennox ordered a hot beef sandwich. That smirk again. Was Cathy this competitive with all women?

Lennox thanked her for the meeting.

"You said Jeff's a suspect."

Lennox pulled a regretful face. "Jeff was one of the last people to talk to Hadley. And then, of course, he discovered the body. It looks bad, you know?"

Gone was the smirk replaced by fear. Lennox felt a little ping of satisfaction.

"They won't arrest him, will they?"

"Hard to say," Lennox said. The cops had their man, so unless Lennox could prove Jeff murdered Hadley, he didn't have to worry about jail time. On the Pinocchio meter, Lennox just registered a six.

"Why did Hadley go to Jeff's house in the first place?"

"I don't know," Lennox said. "Do you have any theories?"

Cathy's mouth pinched into a tight little line. She shook her head. Strands of wet hair fell loose from her ponytail. "She went on bothering him. You know, he's worked really hard to get his life back on track."

"Maybe he wanted to help her. They were friends, right?"

"Friendship has to be a two-way street," she said. "You have your friend's best interests at heart."

"Did you ever meet Hadley?" Lennox said.

"No," she said.

"You weren't curious?" Lennox said. "The two of them calling each other all the time?"

"What do you mean 'all the time'? It was hardly ever."

"I've got the phone records for the last year. A lot of phone calls between Jeff and Hadley."

"How many?"

Easy-Peasy to get under this woman's skin. No wonder Jeff knew he had thirty seconds to get off the phone or he'd be hearing about it all night. Hadley must've driven her wild.

Lennox took a soothing tone. "I didn't mean to alarm you. Hadley had a serious boyfriend and Jeff said the two of you are getting married?"

"He did?" Lines fanned out around Cathy's eyes when she smiled. When she smiled, she didn't look like such a cast iron bitch.

The waiter brought Lennox's sandwich.

Lennox pushed it to the side and asked for more tea. After he left, Lennox leaned forward and said in a low voice, "Let's talk about the night of the murder."

Cathy looked at her watch. "I only have a half hour left on my lunch break."

"Plenty of time," Lennox said. "What you can tell me is really important to rule out Jeff as a suspect."

"I don't know much," Cathy said. "He came home early. We made dinner. He read a story to Alex. We watched a show and went to bed at 10:30. Jeff got up early. I was asleep when he left." Cathy's story didn't line up with Jeff's. He said he came to her house at nine, that the kid was asleep. Why hadn't Dick the dick looked into that a little deeper?

"What time do you usually get up?"

"Six."

Lennox noted the time. Jeff had said he left Cathy's around seven. "Did you have breakfast together?"

"He'd already left."

"So, Jeff must've left really early."

Cathy wrapped her hand around her water glass, then realized it was empty.

"Hadley called shortly before ten that night?"

Cathy looked at her watch again. Said that Jeff got a lot of calls at night. "He sells real estate."

"I know. But Jeff said you knew the call was from Hadley. He said he had to get off the phone double-quick or he'd hear about it half the night."

Cathy's face reddened up to the part in her hair. "Jeff doesn't talk that way about me. You made that up."

"C'mon Cathy, it's not a crime to dislike your fiancé's ex-girlfriend."

Fiancé. She loved it.

"Hadley was the one that got him hooked on drugs in the first place," Cathy said. "People who love each other should want them to be the best they can be."

It sounded like a boyfriend remodel to Lennox. Like all the time you were talking about a guy's potential, you're trying to shape him into something else. Like men let you do that.

"Jeff left her almost a year ago," Cathy said in a defiant voice that challenged Lennox to oppose her.

Nine months according to Jeff. What a pair. Lennox wondered which one of them was telling the truth. "But Hadley kept calling him. It's in the phone records."

"He couldn't help it if she called," Cathy said. She checked her watch again. "I have to go back to work," she said.

"Best guess, when do you think Jeff left that morning we're talking about?" Lennox said.

"I don't know."

"You didn't get up in the middle of the night to go to the bathroom?" Lennox said.

There it was: *Busted* written across Cathy's face.

"Yeah, sure, I use the bathroom at night. I don't really wake up."

"Wouldn't you wake up enough to know if Jeff wasn't in bed with you?"

"Maybe I did. I can't remember. I was so tired I just fell back asleep. I take sleep aids for my insomnia. They're prescription."

"May I ask what you take?"

"What does that have to do with anything?" Cathy said. "Look, I have to go. I'm late."

She struggled into her damp jacket and left. She started running the minute she cleared the bistro's door. Cathy. The name conjured teddy bears and cheerleading squads, women marrying young and having kids. Their kids having kids. Grandma Cathy, only too happy to show you the latest pics of the grandkids. Not this Cathy. Not at all.

Lennox poked her fork into the hot beef sandwich. The gravy had congealed on the edges of the plate and the corners of the bread had turned gray. The restaurant was emptying out.

Lennox picked up her pen and scribbled in her notebook a possible scenario. Jeff gets a call from Hadley right before they go to bed, then in the middle of the night he leaves. Those sleep aids Cathy took must really pack a punch. Or Cathy was faking sleep. She would've suspected that Jeff went to see Hadley. What would Cathy have done? What would Lennox have done if she was jealous as hell of her lover's ex? Lennox would've driven over to Jeff's house. To confirm or confront.

But where was Jeff in this scenario? Say he'd partied with Hadley and was passed out somewhere in the house. The ex-girlfriend drunk as a loon and naked lolling in the hot tub. Cathy would be furious. She wanted this man for a husband and a father for her little boy. She was fighting for her family.

• • •

Lennox had just enough time to visit Tomek. She drove downtown to the Multnomah County courthouse where the court was holding Tomek until his trial. The interview room smelled of Lysol, sweat, and a hundred years of trouble. And it was overdue for another coat of gray-white paint. An armed male guard led Tomek to the Formica-topped table. After Tomek sat and the guard was well out of earshot, Lennox asked him how he was.

"You know." He looked down at the table. "Not good."

There was a sag to his face, as if his skin had loosened from his skull. He had a look about him like she'd seen on dogs when they'd been beaten. How they sit there thinking they must've done something wrong and just take it.

"You should have money in your account for stuff."

He nodded. "Yeah. Tell Mom thanks."

"I went to the library and talked to the people who worked with Hadley. They said what a good person she was. How she volunteered to help people learn to read."

"I miss her," he said in a tiny voice.

"It occurred to me," Lennox said. "Maybe she helped you with your reading?"

"People thought I was too stupid." He let out a long

soggy breath like he'd been crying, but he'd never cry in jail. He knew better.

"I wish I could've met her." Lennox wasn't just blowing smoke up his skirt. But still, she earned a look of trust from Tomek she hadn't seen before. Maybe he would tolerate a more challenging question.

"Hadley was this great lady who helped people, but she liked to do drugs."

"It's kind of like medicine," Tomek said. "For depression, you know?"

"Your mom tell you that?"

He nodded.

"Do you do drugs?" she said.

His face screwed up as if she'd suggested that he ate worms.

"But you sell them to unhappy people," Lennox said.

Yes.

"There was the remains of a speedball by the hot tub where Hadley was found," she said. "Did you bring her that?"

"I didn't bring her anything." His fingers crawled up to his mouth. Classic tell.

"C'mon, Tomek," she said. "You couldn't come to Hadley earlier, you were making deliveries. She didn't want a piece of that? Your thumbprint was on the packet."

He looked down at the table again.

"I can't help if you won't level with me," she said.

"She wanted some coke," he said in a low voice. "She doesn't do heroin."

"You're sure you've never sold or given Hadley a speedball?"

"She just likes coke," he said.

"So how did your thumbprint end up on that packet?"

He didn't answer. Wouldn't look at her.

"Talk to me, Tomek."

She gave him a moment.

"Yeah," he said.

"Yeah, what?"

"Sometimes we sell that stuff," he mumbled.

"Who do you sell it to?"

"I don't know," he said. "I'm bad with names."

She asked him about the rubber gloves. It was clear he didn't know what she was talking about. His blond-lashed eyes cast down, shoulders slumped forward. It was enough for now.

"Can I bring you anything?" she said.

He raised his eyes to hers. "A book?" he said.

She asked him what he wanted to read. Told him she'd see to it right away. Told him to take care, they'd sort it out. Told him to think about the customers he sold speedballs to. "One of them could've hurt Hadley."

CHAPTER 10

Lennox knew Mary Carson from way back when they were both new to criminal justice, so she was tickled that Mary worked as Tomek Jagoda's parole officer. Mary didn't have time to go out for lunch, go out for a drink, go out for anything. Lennox agreed to meet her at her office in the Mead Building, and Lennox would bring take-out for the two of them.

The floor that housed the county probation department was set up like a honeycomb, the center packed with file cabinets, surrounded by small glass-fronted offices. Four parole officers, dressed in Halloween costumes, pulled files from the drawers. A cat, a vampire, an oompa loompa, a devil. Through the glass wall, Lennox saw that Mary was deep in conversation with a skinny boy. The kid had dust brown hair and ink running from the throat of his hoodie over his chin. He looked like he should still be in high school.

Three chairs were lined up outside Mary's office. Lennox sat listening to the low murmur of conversation between

Mary and her client. The smell of garlic, hot pepper, and fried food rose from the sack of General Tso's chicken.

The door opened and the kid shuffled out, smelling like he'd slept in his unwashed clothes.

"Lennox, c'mon in," Mary said, large jack-o'-lantern earrings swinging nearly to her shoulders. "You look great. You haven't aged a bit."

Lennox returned the compliment.

Mary patted her wide hips. "I've gotten fat," she said. "Between this job and the kids, we live on take-out. Adam doesn't seem to mind."

Kids. A husband who didn't mind if you gained twenty pounds. *Don't want what you don't have*, she'd read somewhere. But if you don't want something, how are you ever going to get it? They opened the cartons of take-out and broke apart their chopsticks.

"Tomek Jagoda," Lennox said.

Mary reached his file from the side of her desk. "You know his record, right?"

"Possession, intent to sell," Lennox said.

Mary speared a piece of deep fried chicken. Talked with her mouth full. "He's sweet. Genuinely sweet. That's one thing you can't fake."

Maybe that was true. Lennox tried to think of all the sweet people she'd ever known. Sweet wasn't a trait she ran across often.

"That family of his. Poor guy never had a chance. But try telling him his family's no good, that they're just using him."

Lennox got a blot of orange grease on her notebook. "Did he tell you about his girlfriend?"

"The librarian," Mary said. "After her death, he comes in here. Tears. Tells me I'm the only one that understands."

"Understands what, exactly?"

"What a good person she was. How much he loved her and she loved him."

"What if he found the librarian naked in another man's house," Lennox said. "Then what?"

"You mean would he hurt her?" Mary said. She munched another bite of food as she gave the thought some serious play. "I don't think so," she said.

An old man pressed his skinny face against the glass of Mary's office. Bloodshot eyes, army fatigues. "My twelve-thirty," she said. She held her finger up signaling one minute and turned to Lennox. "Remember that story about the judge whose wife caught him with a hooker? Told the wife 'It's not me.' Tomek's the kind of guy who'd believe it."

Lennox stood up, gave Mary a hug.

"We miss Fulin," Mary said in a low voice and patted Lennox on the back.

"Lesbians!" the grizzled man shouted on the other side of the glass.

It took a loon like that guy to dissolve the rock in Lennox's gut every time Fulin's name was mentioned. She swallowed and thanked Mary for her time. Promised they'd get together soon, knowing perfectly well that with a full-time job, a husband and three kids, who knew when they were going to get together.

Lennox swung by her house and wrote up her notes. Mary had confirmed what Lennox had been feeling since her first visit with Tomek. Edged lawn, a dozen bird feeders, and a bookcase full of fantasy. The photo of him and Hadley, both of them smiling, lots of teeth. Hadley was a pretty woman. Shoulder-length dark hair, petite. Lennox got what Tomek saw in her. And he was a good-looking guy if you liked linemen, and he adored her. And he could supply her with enough cocaine to keep her happy. Only she wasn't happy. She had Slocum, Ito, and some mysterious Terry Purcell character in tow. That's the thing about coke: it's never enough.

CHAPTER 11

Why did Hadley call Dr. Slocum on his personal phone the night of her murder? Hadley could've blackmailed him, could've been sleeping with him and he'd grown tired of her. She'd become a nuisance. She called Slocum the night she was murdered, and he showed up ready to OD her. Instead he found her in the tub and drowned her ass.

Slocum had located his clinic in a busy Beaverton intersection, across the street from a large mall and catty corner to a procession of little strip malls. Beaverton was Chain Store City as far as the eye could see. The residential neighborhoods were ranch houses. People tended to favor shrubs. The tallest tree in anyone's landscape was twelve foot and skinny. Sidewalks were rare. But, depending on traffic, you could hop on the freeway and you were downtown in minutes.

Lennox signed the check-in sheet at Slocum's clinic and was handed a stack of pages for her to check and sign. The waiting room was decorated in a soothing combination of sage green and eggplant. Muted temple music played in the background. Close her eyes and...she was still in Beaverton. Leafing through a magazine, Lennox tried to suss out the clientele. Never in her life had she been in a healthier waiting room. No one coughed, no jaws were clenched, no bodies doubled over; there were no pained expressions.

Lennox waited forty minutes before a large redhead in shamrock green scrubs called her name. Her weight, blood pressure, and temperature were recorded. She was shown a laminated card illustrating a series of lollipop heads from one to ten: one with a big smile, no pain; ten an upside-down smile with tears running down its lollipop cheeks. Pain was something Lennox was very familiar with. For the last year she hadn't been able to make it through the night without taking Advil, and after a day on her feet, she walked with a limp. Every moment she spent in pain reminded her of Fulin. Fulin, her dear friend, her partner, gone for good.

The nurse left Lennox with instructions to undress. She sat, her bare butt sticking to the paper liner on the exam table, a tent-sized hospital gown draped over the front of her. The neck hole of the gown slipped off her shoulder. She ran her finger up the jagged length of her scar from knee to armpit, the places along her flank where the flesh dipped and puckered. The scar had healed to an ugly white line. A long bitter reminder of how stupid she had been. Fulin was gone, and she had a zipper up her flank.

Fruitless to go over it again, how she should've trusted her gut. That was the diabolical thing about hope: it made you override your instincts, overlook the laws of probability. It made you believe in luck, and that's not how luck works. Lennox plucked a *Star* magazine from the wall rack and wondered what this Dr. Slocum was like in the flesh.

She knew what he looked like on paper. He owned his

own practice. He'd run afoul of the medical board four years before for prescribing a controlled substance not in accordance with treatment principles. He beat the rap without repercussions. Fifty-six years old, ten years single after a fifteen-year marriage. Slocum had two children, the younger one still in college, and he continued to pay a hefty sum in child support. He owned a house in the West Hills. Zillow.com pegged it at two-million-two. His BMW was a year old. His new wife, Abby, drove a brand new Jag.

Lennox penciled it out. The dude needed 34K a month just to make his payments, and that's if he lived on peanut butter.

She shifted her weight to her right cheek on the exam table. Slocum had been questioned about the Hadley Eberhart murder. He and his wife had driven Friday night after work to Timberline Lodge. They'd stayed there the weekend.

Another slow twenty minutes crawled by before Slocum came through the door. Every one of his fifty-six years showed on his face. He stood short and stocky, his silvered hair in coarse curls. Imagine a cherub pushing sixty, with red-framed glasses, his nose and ears grown longer, his lips fatter.

He shook hands and introduced himself. His hand was cold and dry. Then he perched on a stool and read a computer screen.

"You have pain?" he said. His eyes slid from the computer screen to her face.

"A car accident," she said. She pulled the gown so that her left side was exposed. He didn't look up from the computer at her bare flesh, but rather asked her how long ago the accident occurred. Did she have trouble with her back? Lennox told him her leg ached during the day, woke her up at night.

He asked her what level of pain she had and motioned with his head to the chart of lollipop heads.

She closed the gown. "Eight," she said.

He asked her which pharmacy she preferred. Typed more into the computer. "I'm prescribing OxyContin," he said. "The instructions are on the bottle. Call my office in three days and let me know if that's relieving the pain. The nurse will give you a print-out describing side effects, symptoms to watch out for. You may run into some constipation taking this drug. Prune juice works for most patients. Any questions?"

"Can I drive on it?" she said.

He stopped typing and made eye contact. "I wouldn't recommend it."

"But I have pain during the day." She made her voice pitch into a whine.

At last he really looked at her. "What do you want?"

"Is there something that I can take so that I can drive and work and deal with the pain?"

He held her eyes another moment, then went back to clacking on the keyboard. "We'll try you on Adderall. That should keep you focused so that you can take the pain medication."

Tops, he'd spent four minutes with her. He didn't ask her how she'd been dealing with the pain during the last year. Based on a chart of lollipop faces, he'd prescribed a heavy-duty opioid and prescription speed.

"Aren't you even going to examine me?" She slid the gown back to reveal her torso.

He looked annoyed. He turned from the computer

and walked over to the exam table. He smelled like orange peel and some kind of spice. She guessed his cologne was expensive. He must have noticed that she was paying too close attention to him. He took a slight step back. She pointed to where the scar began. His eyes ran the length of her torso down her thigh.

"I can see how that would be painful," he said in a flat voice.

That was it. He didn't check her range of motion. He didn't feel the tissue around her scarring. She barely had time to thank him for the so-called exam before he disappeared behind the exam room door. From what she'd read about pill mills, this looked classic. All Hadley had to do was slip into a hospital gown, tell Slocum she had an owie, and he'd write her a script. But how was he making more money than the average highly paid doctor? Lennox pulled on her jeans and finished getting dressed.

All the way home she chewed on the problem. Questions: what did Slocum write in his patient notes when they were submitted to the insurance company? How did he justify the prescriptions he wrote? Did he inflate the severity of the patient's problem? What about his source? Do pharmaceutical companies flag a clinic that orders large amounts of OxyContin? Maybe he used street suppliers. Lennox wondered if the Jagodas were acquainted with the doc. She could ask Idzi.

• • •

It started raining harder. A semi blew past her truck in the next lane and splashed a bucket's worth of water against her windshield. Slocum was unwilling to look at her naked body. It left her feeling shamed somehow. Had she changed so much in the last year that men no longer looked at her with any interest? There was the poker game last Friday when she might as well have been invisible. Did she want men to leer at her? She wasn't thinking straight.

Lennox stopped at the drugstore before driving home. The rain halted as she pulled in the driveway and climbed her porch steps. The beagle next door bayed like his heart had broken. The air smelled of dead leaves and wood smoke. She held her breath as she jiggled the key in the lock. Ever since Idzi had broken into her house, Lennox felt jumpy.

By seven that night, Lennox had refined her notes on Dr. Slocum and figured out a plan going forward. Thirty-six OxyContins to be taken every four hours as needed for pain made it six days' worth. First step, call his office and tell him the pills weren't taking away the pain. See what he did next. He must know that the pharmacy would question a fistful of prescriptions. If she pushed him, would he sell her drugs?

If he did overprescribe, then Lennox could see how Hadley could've blackmailed him. Hadley went to Slocum, blamed him for her addiction. Threatened to register a complaint. Lennox made a mental note to see if she could go deeper with Slocum's trouble with the medical board.

She stood up to stretch and take the half-eaten tray of microwaved chicken parmigiana to the compost pail when her phone rang. Shawn Boyd, the cute cop from the courthouse calling. He asked her if she'd come and have a drink with him.

"I have to work," she said.

"One drink," he said with a coaxing voice. A cute guy asking her out. But no. She had work to do.

"I'm swamped," she said.

"One drink in your neighborhood," he said. "I'll have you back in less than an hour. Hour and a half, tops."

There was so much to do. There was always so much to do. Lennox felt her shoulders relax and drop. Why not?

"Okay," she said.

CHAPTER 12

Discovery had overtaken the space in Lennox's tiny home office, so she had moved everything into the dining room. Which was a problem because Idzi was coming over for a round of questioning. Lennox threw a bed sheet over the stacks of discovery she'd sorted on the dining room table. Turned the bulletin board so that it faced the wall.

Idzi rang Lennox's doorbell like a proper visitor.

The minute Idzi stepped inside Lennox's door, her attention veered to the lumps beneath the sheet. It was like Oz. Don't look behind the curtain.

"What do you got there?" Idzi said. "A body?"

Lennox helped Idzi out of her coat and ushered her to the chair by the fireplace. Idzi was turned out as always: boutique clothes, expensive shoes, that goddamn crocodile handbag. But all of that couldn't cover up her drawn face. She was worried about her boy, and by the looks of it not getting enough food or sleep.

Once Idzi was settled in her chair, Lennox opened her notebook.

"What's that for?" Idzi motioned with her chin to the notebook.

"I have some questions for you."

"That bulletin board over there?" Idzi said.

Lennox felt herself pinned with those blackbird eyes. Not much got past the old woman. "Suspects," Lennox said.

"It's blank," Idzi said. "You don't have anyone yet?"

"I'm not working for you any longer. Remember?" Lennox said. "I saw Tomek yesterday."

Idzi's face softened and opened up. "How is he?"

"Okay," Lennox said. "It helps that he knows the drill. He said some things about Hadley."

Idzi shrugged. "He'll get over her."

"He admitted that he was skimming off you to provide Hadley with her coke habit." Now it was Lennox's turn to pin Idzi in her gaze.

"My boy wouldn't do that."

Lennox knew when she was being stonewalled. "That was the problem with Hadley, wasn't it?" Lennox said. "Tomek didn't listen to you like he used to. Then he started stealing from you. How long had it been going on?"

"You're going to put my picture on your bulletin board?" Idzi said.

"Just answer the question."

Idzi hiked her shoulders in a dismissive gesture. Stealing, shmealing. Lennox wasn't buying it.

"You can't control your oldest boy," she said to Idzi. "Pieter has his own family. But Tomek. It's like you said, he's an innocent. Then you lost him to Hadley."

"I never lost him," Idzi said. "You don't know our family well enough to say things like that."

"Where were you the night of October 9th?"

"I am going up on your board." Idzi nodded. How many times had Aurora nodded with that same weary face? *I'm disappointed in you.* Lennox was pretty much immune to it.

"Why would I have hired you if I'd drowned the librarian?" Idzi said.

"It happens all the time. Haven't you heard? The first one on the scene that calls the cops is the lead suspect."

"Get my coat," Idzi told her. "We're done here."

"I'd like to write you off, but how can I when you clearly have a motive and you don't answer my questions?" Lennox walked over to Idzi's chair. Made her look up. "First tell me where you were the night of."

"I was with the old man like I am every night. He falls asleep in his chair about nine o'clock. At ten, I wake him up and we go to bed."

This was the first time Lennox had heard of Mr. Jagoda Senior. "Tell me," she said. "Is he in the business as well?"

"No. He's an old man. He sits and sleeps." Idzi pushed herself out of her chair. "Get my coat."

"How about Pieter?" Lennox said. "Did you send him over to Ito's house to take care of the Hadley problem?"

Her eyes, her mouth, and her jaw hardened and stayed hard. "That's the way it's going to be," she said. "One way or another someone in our family's going to be convicted for that woman's death."

"I have other suspects," Lennox said. "It's just that I can't rule you and Pieter out."

The old lady waved a dismissive hand.

Lennox watched her leave the house and drive away in her cute little Volkswagen the color of a robin's egg. Then Lennox retrieved Idzi's and Pieter's photos and pinned them back on her board.

CHAPTER 13

Lennox woke up shivering. By the time she got to the bottom of the stairs, she saw why. Her front door was wide open to the weather, the furnace struggling mightily to heat the whole neighborhood. The Jagodas. Crime scene photos, autopsy reports, interviews were strewn across her dining room floor. The bulletin board ripped from the dining room wall, the photos of Idzi and Pieter missing.

Pieter had left his calling card: a ten-inch hunting knife sunk deep in her beautiful dining room table. Her nerves jittered along her spine. She'd bet it was the same knife Pieter had threatened her and Tomek with when she first met him.

Lennox raced to her office and grabbed Old Ugly from her desk drawer, fed the magazine, and racked the slide. Cocked and locked. She walked down the hallway, into Fulin's old bedroom. It still smelled like sandalwood incense. She edged the closet door open, ready to shoot if she had to. The closet was empty except for a pair of his jeans and his turquoise leather jacket.

She opened the main hall closet, checked the living room, the kitchen. The back door was still barred and the windows secured. Lennox took a deep breath and opened the door leading to the basement. A bare bulb at the bottom of the stairs lit the shadows. She crouched on each step as she descended and tried to penetrate the gloom. She felt cold air spilling from the broken window before she saw the sawn-through, one-half-inch tubular steel bars and the broken glass.

Lennox called her handyman to repair the basement window before she made her first pot of coffee. Then she called Idzi. But the old lady didn't pick up. She didn't pick up the next seven times Lennox tried her number, either.

This called for a visit to Marie's Bakery. Lennox tucked Old Ugly in the back of her jeans, her pepper spray in her front pocket. No matter how they tried to intimidate her, Lennox would find Hadley's murderer. The sun pierced Lennox's windshield and made her wince as she drove southeast. She'd mislaid her sunglasses sometime in September when the skies had last been clear. Banners snapped in the wind on the top of the auto parts store on the corner of Cesar Chavez and Yamhill. Pedestrians walked with their heads down and their collars up. Lennox parked her truck across the street from Marie's Bakery and ran into the shop. The blast of warmth and hot bread aroma made her feel welcome. That lasted a couple of seconds.

"I need to talk to Idzi now," Lennox said in a voice loud enough that every customer stopped mid-chew to stare at her.

"Idzi's not here," the counter woman said.

"Call her. Tell her to get over here."

The woman pulled a phone from the pocket of her

waitress uniform and a moment later started speaking Polish. She re-pocketed the phone.

"You wait outside," she said to Lennox, her head nodding in the direction of the door.

"I'll wait right here," Lennox said. Lennox had asked for Idzi, but she knew she was getting Pieter. She pulled the pepper spray from her pocket and held it close to her thigh. She was ready if Pieter wanted to make it physical.

The eight tables and two booths were all taken by gawping customers. She slid into the closest booth across from an elderly couple. They struggled to exit. Maybe it was mean to take over someone's space. Lennox wasn't feeling too kindly toward the Polish community at present. An old woman in a flowered head scarf and ankles as big as Lennox's thighs shook her head in disapproval, crumbs flying from her lips.

The bakery began to empty. Each time someone left, the wind caught the glass door and bounced it against its hinges. A cold draft of air invaded the warmth.

Most of the next ten minutes were spent glaring and being glared at. If dirty looks were lasers, Lennox and the counter woman would've been two piles of ash. Lennox sweated like she'd run five miles. The woman reached under the counter and retrieved a brown plastic tub. She bussed and wiped down the vacated tables. Heavy china clinked against the silverware as she went from table to table. Only one table was still occupied: the old woman with the flowered scarf.

A sudden gust of wind rattled the plate glass window and the door flew open. Pieter Jagoda stepped into the bakery, unshaven and reeking of cigarette smoke. He spotted Lennox in a red-hot second and crossed the room.

The counter woman Lennox had been exchanging dirty looks with disappeared into the kitchen. Lennox's heart beat wildly against her chest. Pieter grabbed her by the upper arm and hauled her out of the booth just like she figured he would. Before he could reach her other arm, she swung it around and blasted him in the face with the pepper spray.

He let go of her and collapsed to his knees, coughing his lungs out, tears and snot streaming down the front of his sweatshirt. She jumped away from him and watched the sonofabitch writhe on the floor. There was nothing sweeter than taking down a bully.

"Stay out of my house," she said. And left the bakery.

Retaliation is a dish best served not at all. Tit for tat was not getting her any closer to solving the Eberhart murder, and it made living in her own house impossible. But she couldn't *not* react to being pushed around. If she let herself be cowed by these people she might as well hang up her gumshoes and teach third grade.

Driving north through the neighborhoods of Clinton and Hawthorne, she called Ham. Asked him if he had time for a cocktail.

"Eleven in the morning's a little early for me," he said.

Eleven? It felt like closing time. She was exhausted, and admittedly scared. A gust of wind blew her truck sideways.

"Coffee, then," she said. She told Ham she needed his sage counsel. Needed it now. She knew that giving Lennox Cooper advice had to figure in Ham's top ten favorite things. He agreed to meet her at the Shanty.

Ham sat alone at a table nursing a cup of coffee when Lennox entered the bar. The Shanty was dark and snug. A smear of sunlight came from the one window. The low drone of television and the hiccup of a video poker machine were the only sounds. Lennox ordered a Jack and Coke and joined him.

"What's up?" he said. Lennox took in his steady accountant eyes, pale blue Oxford shirt, and navy patterned tie. Here was a guy whose judgment you'd readily trust.

She began by telling him about Pieter's threats, Idzi's anger, and this latest episode where someone broke into her house and assaulted her furniture.

His eyes widened with concern. "I told you not to work out of your house, that you needed to carry. What's the matter with you?"

"I am now," she said. "Wait a minute, there's more."

Ham got redder and visibly more upset as she concluded with pepper spraying Pieter.

"I don't get it," she said. "Idzi wanted to hire me, so why does she break into my house instead of waiting in her car like a normal person until I got home? And why did Pieter break in last night? Don't they see that they're making themselves look guilty?"

"They're bullying you," Ham said.

"That part I get, but why?"

"You've got to get an office," Ham said. "Not someday. Now."

"That's fixing the barn door after the horse has bolted. Here's the irony—the signing bonus Idzi paid me would've gotten me a downtown office."

"You didn't mention any signing bonus," Ham said.

"That's because I gave it back," she said. "I'm working for Kline now. You haven't answered my question. Why?"

"It's obvious. They want you to pin the murder on anyone but them. And now you're not safe." He leaned forward. "Move in with us. I mean it, kid. Today."

"I'm not leaving my house," Lennox said. "They're not going to scare me off."

"Are you nuts? They sunk a knife in your table while you were sleeping."

"I can't stay in your guest room. How am I going to get any work done?"

"Well, you can't keep this up," he said.

Neither one of them spoke. Ham sipped his coffee, shook his head, then sipped more coffee. Lennox listened to the blip of the video poker machine, trying to think of a way to continue her investigation and keep the Jagodas off her back.

"How about this?" Ham said. "Stay with 2-K. He's rattling around in that big old house his folks left him. You'd have a room and police protection."

She knew she wasn't safe. She hadn't been safe since she set up shop in her own home. Her house. She'd worked her ass off to make the down payment on that property. And it had appreciated, the whole neighborhood becoming a hot place to live. It was the one wise move she could point to and feel proud of. And now she was supposed to surrender it. She wouldn't.

Ham whipped out his phone and dialed 2-K, told him that Lennox was in a jam and that she wasn't safe until this murder investigation was over. 2-K said sure. Said he'd be home by six, and she could move in tonight.

"You're a good man, Sidney." First time Lennox had ever heard Ham use 2-K's God-given name. "That's settled," Ham said. "Drink up, Lennox. I'm driving you to your house to get your stuff."

"You don't have to do that," she said. "And I've got more work to do this afternoon."

"You mean after pepper spraying the Jagoda guy, you've got more in mind?"

"You know what's funny?" Lennox said. "I've come up with five solid suspects, but none of the five were even listed as persons of interest in the discovery. Don't you think that's weird?"

"Who's the investigator?"

"Dick the dick."

"Wasn't he—?"

"Yeah," she said. "Tommy's partner for a while. That doesn't mean he's dirty. But he's got that same Tommy attitude: the easiest answer is the right answer."

Two years back, Tommy had been caught disappearing evidence. That and his overall sloppy police work got him busted down to patrol. Lennox used to love Tommy, back when he was still married and promising to leave his wife for her. Now she wouldn't have him on a stick.

Ham finished his coffee. Said goodbye. "2-K's expecting you at six? Right?"

"Right," she said. "And thanks, Ham."

How many questions had Dick the dick left unanswered once he had Tomek in his sights? She phoned Central Precinct.

Dick picked up his phone on the third ring.

"Officer Sloane," she said.

"What do you want, Cooper?"

"I thought I could buy you a beer, pick your brain about this Jagoda thing."

"I don't drink."

"Coffee then?"

"We've got a coffeepot here and I got a mountain of paperwork. Nice talking to ya."

Click.

His phone manners were on par with his interviewing skills. Dickish. Leastways, she knew he was at work. She hopped in the Bronco and headed to the station. Lennox hated going to Central. The place had sunny windows and the smell of burnt coffee and was crawling with cops all on the same team, the good guys fighting the bad guys. Coming to Central made her feel like a lonely little onion in a petunia patch.

She found Dick stooped over his laptop in a narrow cubicle. She said howdy. Dick tipped up his long horse head and made frowning eye contact with her.

"I told you I was busy," he said.

"Yeah, this has to do with work," she said. "I'm on the defense team representing Tomek Jagoda."

He gave her a smug half-smile. "Figures," he said.

Dick was improving her mood. Good vs. evil came into perspective talking to a guy like Dick the dick. She figured she had two good questions before he threw her out, so she led with Dr. Slocum and why he wasn't a person of interest.

"Why would he be?"

"He prescribed OxyContin to the murder victim. You know, Oxys? They've been in the news a lot lately?"

"Don't get snotty with me, Cooper," he said. "I answer to the prosecutor, not you."

"Fair enough. One more question, for old time's sake." Old times. He hadn't liked her when she'd dated Tommy. He liked her even less when she'd become a PI. But Lennox had to believe she'd won at least a grudging respect from him. In case after case, without the resources and backing of the police bureau, she'd proved to be the better investigator.

"Terry Purcell," she said. "The victim called Terry's number the night of her murder. Who is he?"

Dick took a deep breath, let it out noisily. "There is no Terry Purcell. The phone number is disconnected. Our best guess is it's some druggie using a burner phone and an alias."

"You didn't try to track it down?"

"Track down a burner phone? We look like the NSA here?" he said. "I gotta go back to work."

He turned his attention back to the laptop, hit a bunch of keys to wake it up. "Good seeing you recovered and all," he mumbled to the computer screen.

Did she really hear that? Maybe he was a better guy than she gave him credit for. "Thanks," she said.

CHAPTER 14

The phone rang against Lennox's cheekbone. It took her a few breaths before she realized she'd done a face plant on her desk and fallen asleep. She sat up straight, fumbled for the call.

Ham.

"Where the hell are you? 2-K's been phoning me since the crack of dawn. You were supposed to be at his house. He said he called and called."

"I must've dozed off," she said. Her mouth felt gummy, her back hurt. Old Ugly was digging into the waistband of her jeans, probably leaving a permanent imprint. How late had she worked?

"You got some kind of death wish?" Ham said.

She told him she'd been working, poring over the files. It got late. "I tried staying over there," she said. "His buddies come over, they drink beer and play pinball in the living room until 2:00 in the morning. I was sleeping in his mother's bedroom. It smells like an old lady."

Ham told her he'd found an office for her. Quimby and

24th. It was dirt cheap, and had an intercom system and plenty of businesses in the building so that she wouldn't be all alone. They'd hold it for her until ten o'clock. When could she get there? Lennox asked him what time it was.

Seven in the morning. And Ham was already fully caffeinated. She told him she could get there at eight or she could have breakfast and meet him at eight-thirty.

"Eat your bagel," he said. "I'll call the manager, set it up. 8:30. Look respectable. And call 2-K before he has a cow."

Lennox showed up at 8:20 in her interview clothes and met Ham outside the office building on the corner of 24th.

"You brought your checkbook, your credit cards, right?" Ham said.

"Yeah, which building is it?"

Ham jerked his head in the direction of a huge, dark gray bungalow on the corner. It had a wide porch that faced the street. It looked like the kind of place that had built-in bookcases and tile on the floors.

"Not that one?"

He nodded.

"I can't afford that."

"Are you carrying?" Ham said. Like he was asking her if she brought her homework.

"What do you want me to do? Shoot the property manager if she doesn't rent to me?"

"You're hopeless," Ham said.

"I'm kidding. What happened to your sense of humor?"

"You," he said.

Lennox didn't pursue what he meant. She didn't want to know.

A young woman with raven black hair in khaki slacks

and a navy blazer hurried down the sidewalk towards them in the weak October light.

Ham muttered under his breath, "What's that shmutzka on her face?"

"A nose ring," Lennox whispered. Geez, her hands were clammy. You'd think she was applying for a job.

"Goes nice with the blazer," Ham said.

"Sorry I'm late," the property manager said. "The parking. You know how it is."

Yeah, Lennox knew how it was. There was no such thing as off-street parking in the alphabet district. Burnside to Vaughn, residents vied with shoppers and merchants to find a naked curb anywhere close to their destination.

"Where are you located now?" the property manager asked. Her name was Lisa.

"Northeast Portland," Lennox said. "52nd and Broadway."

"Well, you're moving to the right side of the river," Lisa said. West-siders, man, they were so full of themselves. Before Lennox could weigh in on the east-west debate, Ham jumped in, asking what was needed to secure the office.

"I haven't seen it yet," Lennox said.

Lisa smiled. "Is he your brother?"

"Feels like it," Lennox said.

They were ushered up a steep flight of cement steps from the street to the front porch. A small entry led down a narrow hallway with oak floors, oak woodwork. Lennox's would-be office was at the far end of the hallway on the first floor. They passed an insurance office, an acupuncturist. Lisa waved a large ring of keys and unlocked two separate locks. The office was the size of Lennox's dining room. She could house both her desk and a work table, two visitor chairs and her rubber tree. There was a closet with built-in shelves for paper and office supplies. There was a bathroom down the hall.

"How much?" Lennox said.

A thousand a month, the property manager said. It had natural woodwork, the kind they don't finish houses with anymore, and lath and plaster, fresh paint the color of cafe au lait. It was a steal for this neighborhood. The office window looked out on big two-story high trees with just enough leaves left to identify them as maples. Catty-corner was the Stepping Stone Cafe. There was coffee across the street and lunch if she had any spare money. It was a real office.

Could she consistently make the payment without living on ramen the rest of her life?

Ham shifted weight from foot to foot. She knew he could sense her hesitancy. "We'll take it," he blurted.

• • •

Lennox got to the Steel Bridge before she realized she was grinning like an idiot. Her own office. She felt excited and scared shitless. How was she going to afford her mortgage, a rental, and Friday night poker? She'd rather teach school or sell shoes than give up poker. But she wouldn't have to give up the game, so long as she kept on winning. And she liked ramen.

Her own office. It was like graduating or getting married, at least the way she imagined getting married would feel like. And she would be safer, that was for sure. Three years and how many break-ins? Not to mention her old partner's kid vandalizing the shit out of her house. If her home address wasn't splashed all over her advertising, maybe she'd have some peace. She'd be safer. It had been tough going ever since the Portland Police fired her ass. She'd taken some hits, made mistakes. It took some adjustment to go from always having someone watching your back to being alone. And she hadn't the money to get an office and make her mortgage.

Now she'd need new business cards, change her website, everything. Her head was full of what was needed before the guys got there at six to help move her office furniture. She pulled on to 52nd.

Parked in front of her house was a robin egg blue cabriolet. Idzi Jagoda.

She watched Idzi struggle out of the driver's seat and trot stiffly towards Lennox. By the time she reached the porch, the old lady was red-faced and winded.

"You wanted to see me," Idzi said.

"That's right." Lennox led her to the dining room. They stood eye-to eye, neither of them willing to sit down before the other. Lennox pointed to the gash in the table.

"What you did to Pieter at the bakery was assault," Idzi said. "I have witnesses."

"Go ahead, call it in," Lennox said. "My story is that it was self-defense. He had his hands on me. Let's get something clear right now. You can't bully your way out of this. You and Pieter are suspects. If you're innocent, why don't you cooperate? Give me solid alibis, turn over your phone logs."

"I'm not going to do that," the old lady said. "You're not a cop. There's nothing you can do to us."

"Tomek was in love with Hadley," Lennox said. "You could've done the murder yourself. She was so wasted, anyone could've drowned her."

"And framed Tomek?"

"I only have your word that you're not throwing him to the cops to save yourself." Because everything about the old woman was false. How was Lennox going to believe anything she said?

"That's what you believe?" Idzi was red to her hairline.

Lennox was finally getting it, why Idzi had hired her in the first place, why she broke in instead of making an appointment like a regular person.

"You hired me because you're sure Tomek killed Hadley," Lennox said. "Were you looking for him that night? Did he come to you, beg you to help him?"

"You're the detective," Idzi said.

"Is that a yes?" Lennox said. Now it was Lennox turning red. She could feel the flush move over her face, her scalp tingling. Tomek couldn't have killed Hadley. She was so used to meeting with Idzi's resistance that once she quit defending Tomek, Lennox fell flat on her face.

Idzi smoothed her coat, bent over, reached for her crocodile handbag, and walked out the door.

Honestly, what did Lennox expect? What kind of woman engages her children in the drug trade? One thing was clear, the Jagodas weren't going to cooperate. At least Lennox served notice that she wasn't backing down.

Lennox could no longer pretend that her house was safe. She retrieved her sleeping bag from the basement, chucked it into the cab of her truck. Her travel bag from 2-K's was still in the foot well. After the guys finished moving her office furniture, she'd camp there.

CHAPTER 15

After three nights sleeping on the floor of her office, Lennox's body was one big ache. At twenty, she could've slept upside down in her stationary closet, no problem. She was too old for this shit. The upside was that no one broke in and sunk a hunting knife in her desk. She was safe. Only Ham knew she was bivouacked here. Her hair was damp from washing it in the bathroom sink. At eight in the morning the building was still quiet except for the radiators clicking on and off, the Gorge wind beating against the windows. Her intercom buzzed.

"Figured you'd be here at your new digs," August Kline said. "Let me in. I've got coffee."

Ham had snitched her out.

"I'm not unpacked. This isn't a good time." She panicked. Her stuff was everywhere: clothes slung on hangers over the closet door, toiletries lined up on the window sill.

"I'm standing here," Kline said. "In the cold." Like this

was the worst breach of conduct he'd ever experienced, and he was a criminal lawyer for God's sake.

"First floor, end of the hall." Was that her voice squeaking? She buzzed him in. And mashed her sleeping bag under the bottom shelf of her closet.

His sturdy silhouette stood on the other side of the glass door. She let him in and offered him a visitor chair, but he remained standing.

He set the two coffees on her desk and strolled around the office, nodding in approval. If he noticed her shampoo bottle behind the coffeemaker on top of the file cabinet, he didn't react. His suit was well cut; his shoes were shiny. He always looked elegant, which is hard to pull off when you're short. She ought to know.

He stood looking out the window at the trees and the traffic, then over at her bulletin board, which was covered with photos of Idzi, Pieter, Jeff, Cathy and Doc Slocum. He read the index cards pinned beneath each photo.

"So the night of the murder Ito and the Jagodas were home with their respective mates," he said.

"Yeah. I don't know about Dr. Slocum, yet."

"Terry Purcell remains a mystery?"

"Detective Sloane ran into a dead end with Purcell," she said.

"Detective Sloane," he nodded and grinned. "I'm happy you're giving Dick some respect."

"Yeah, well, I'm not giving up so easily on this Terry Purcell character."

"Good. So. Your first office. How does it feel?"

"Great. I guess." She swallowed. "It's a big step."

He looked puzzled. Probably the last time he had to

worry about money was college days. Had he seen her deodorant on the window sill?

She motioned to the visitor chair. He finally sat down, and she was finally able to relax.

"Before I forget, I've got an invite for you," he said. He reached in the pocket of his suit jacket and produced an ivory envelope. Top quality stationery, of course. "It's a fundraiser for literacy my partners and I are throwing."

She thanked him and reached for her scissors, slit the envelope open.

"Portland Art Museum," Lennox said. "Thanks."

"Cocktails, little tapas. Wear a dress. You have a dress, don't you?"

"Of course," she said. She had a little black dress that would knock the eyeballs out of his head.

"And bring a date if you like," Kline said.

"Thanks," she said. For a minute there, she'd seen herself impressing him with her feminine wiles. Now she felt disappointed, somehow.

Kline folded his hands on her desk. "A little bird tells me that the Jagodas have been giving you trouble."

"Nothing I can't handle," she said, thinking about how she was going to get even with that little bird.

"They've broken into your house twice, the last time fatally stabbing your dining room table. Did you call the police?"

"I've taken care of it," she said.

"Camping out in your office. That's how you've taken care of it? The police could have lifted prints off the knife."

"It's Pieter's knife. I'd seen it before."

"Now I'm reassured."

"What if I was a dude?" she said. "Would you be so concerned about my ability to handle this?"

"I don't know." His gray eyes dropped from her face over her breasts, but then he must've realized what he was doing. His ears turned pink. There was an awkward moment. He finally said, "You're not a dude."

That was the thing about this business, about life. It all came down to breasts. And balls. What was courageous in a guy was reckless in a woman. People tried to push her around, and if she pushed back she had a death wish.

"I'll be goddamned if I'll let anybody bully me," she said.

"You can't camp here indefinitely," Kline said. It didn't take a detective to figure out she was holed up here. "I've got just the thing to keep the Jagodas from breaking in. I'll be at your house at six tonight."

"Maybe I have plans," she said.

He looked annoyed. "Do you?"

She made a pretense of looking at her schedule. "I guess six would work out."

"Good."

Poof. He was gone. Kline paying her a visit this morning, then planning on going to her house at six tonight meant he must really be concerned about her safety. He'd invited her to his charity thing. So maybe he thought of her beyond their work relationship.

How could she think that? Bring a date, he'd said. The one thing she'd learned from Tommy was what happens when you get romantic with a co-worker.

All the cops knew that she and Tommy had been sleeping together. She hadn't cared what they knew or what they said behind her back. It ended with her partner shot dead, her fired from the police bureau, and Tommy dropping her like a hot rock.

Kline though, Kline wasn't a co-worker exactly. He was a lawyer. Fraternizing with a lowly PI was slumming. Maybe she had it wrong, maybe he had joined Ham in fussing about her because she'd done a horseshit job of taking care of herself. Her short body was one long scar.

After Kline left, Lennox called Dr. Slocum.

"It's too early to get refills," he said.

"But I'm in pain," she said.

He warned her about opiate abuse. Told her that the drugs were addictive, that she could face serious health issues. It was like he was reading it off a card the way she had read someone their Miranda rights back in the day. She told him she understood, but the pain was acute. Doctors loved that word: *acute*. Slocum's voice grew lower. "Perhaps we could discuss this."

It turned out he could see her on his lunch hour at Koji's.

Lennox spent the rest of the morning reordering her filing system. Footsteps and muffled voices came through her ceiling from the floor above. She liked the company.

Koji's was a block from his clinic. Slocum was popping a piece of sushi in his mouth as she walked in the door. When he saw her, he laid the chopsticks on the side of his plate and watched her fake a limp down the narrow aisle between the counter and the tiny tables against the wall. She did her best to look pained. He told her he wanted cash only. Three-hundred bucks for fifteen pills. She studied his face across the table from her, looked at his pupils, his facial muscles. All she could smell was his expensive cologne, nothing that indicated drug abuse. It seemed that money was his drug of choice. He told her where the nearest ATM was.

As she left Koji's, the new bottle of painkillers rattling in her bag, it occurred to her that she wanted Slocum to be the perp. She could imagine the scenario: the guy over-prescribing opiates to Hadley. Months of that, maybe years. Hadley tells him, *you over-prescribed and now I'm addicted.* How many times did murder come down to a blackmail scheme where the blackmail victim turns on his persecutor?

Lennox spent the rest of the afternoon back at the office researching Slocum's run-in with the medical association. There were more footsteps and voices from upstairs. It beat the ringing silence at her house. Ham had said that Lennox had a death wish. Was his opinion a question of sexism, or was there something more there? Maybe this work was too much for her. But what else would she do? The windows grew darker and it began to hail.

At five o'clock, Lennox drove home. The hail had turned to rain. Her poor little house looked deserted. She unarmed the insecure security. It had been three days. The house was cool, and at the same time stale. She turned up the thermostat and made a pot of coffee. It still didn't feel like enough. She built a fire in the fireplace, burned a stick of sandalwood incense in front of the little brass Ganesh on Fulin's dresser. She rubbed the statue's elephant trunk and his little pot belly for luck.

Better.

Six o'clock on the button the doorbell rang, and there was Kline on her porch with the shadow of a beard on his chin and cheeks. It softened the always professional Kline. She threw the door open. Beside him stood a dog. A big dog. A Nazi dog. A Rottweiler.

"Lennox, meet Gretchen," Kline said.

What the hell? Kline had a dog?

"Come in," she said. "You can tie it out here." She waved her hand in the direction of the animal.

"You don't get it," Kline said. Was she supposed to invite the Nazi canine into her house? She had zero experience with dogs, or any pets for that matter. And now this creature was shedding hair on her porch.

The dog followed Kline into the living room, its claws clicking like dice on Lennox's hardwood floor. Kline sat down on the sofa. The dog flopped on the rug by his feet. Kline wore faded jeans and a ratty brown sweater. He looked great. Smiling, he scratched the dog behind its ears. The animal was bigger than Lennox's mother and smelled.

"Gretchen's better than any security system. Aren't you, girl?" he said in a peculiar sing-song voice. "You won't let the bad guys hurt this little gal."

"Little gal?" Lennox leaned forward in her chair.

A deep grumble rose from the Nazi's throat.

"No, Gretchen," Kline said in a stern voice. "She's our friend." He smoothed the hair that had risen along the dog's back. Dog hair drifted down to Lennox's rug.

"So the dog's for me?" She slowly leaned back in her chair, kept her hands by her side. One leap and the dog would rip her throat out. Lennox could see that it might be better to take her chances with the Jagodas. "I appreciate it, Gus. But animals and me—" Lennox shrugged to let him know how hopeless this all was.

"Nonsense. They're like people." His face had softened the way it did when they discussed a case at Higgins after his second martini, but nicer. He said, "Once you've bonded with her, you'll get along great. You get your house back and she'll keep you safe."

Kline spent the next hour explaining how much to feed her, how much to exercise her. Fresh water was vital. "In fact, Gretchen's probably thirsty now, aren't you, girl?" He used that baby-talk voice again.

They walked into the kitchen together. He asked Lennox for a bowl, then pulled the biggest one Lennox owned out of the cupboard, filled it with water, and set it in front of the stove. Gretchen lapped up half of it. The dog grinned, a toothy grin, water dripping from its enormous teeth.

"See, you want to talk to her. Just like a person," he said. He looked good in jeans. Damned good, actually.

Then he went out to his car and brought in a dog bed.

"Your bedroom's upstairs?" he said.

She must have looked stupefied. She *was* stupefied. "Easiest way to bond with your dog is to have her sleep with you," he told Lennox. Yup. The same could be said about bonding with *her*, Lennox could have told him. But she didn't.

"I'll take it," she said. And hauled the bed upstairs. Meanwhile Kline brought in a large sack of food and a canvas bag smelling like beef jerky that had been left in the trunk of a car for a couple of years. She looked inside the bag. Hooves. Brown empty cow hooves.

"What the hell?" she said.

"She loves these," Kline said. "They make her fart, but if you give her one when you go to your office, she'll work on it all day."

"Are you sure this is a good idea?" Lennox said. "You seem so attached to Gretchen. Won't you miss her?"

"She's my sister's dog," he said. "They moved to the

Netherlands and couldn't take her. I live in a condo. You have the room. You run; she runs. You need protection. I figure it's a win-win."

He patted the dog on the top of her head and cupped her chin in his hand, his face level with hers. "Be my good girl. Guard."

He turned away, his hand raised in a goodbye. Lennox and Gretchen looked each other over. A fat string of drool detached from Gretchen's lip and fell on Lennox's good rug.

CHAPTER 16

Lennox had thought hard about whether to blow off Kline's fancy party, but she decided to go. Mostly to prove to Kline that she could wear a cocktail dress with the best of them. Then she called Shawn. "Open bar," she had said. "Count me in," he answered. She told him he had to wear a suit, and he was still game.

Lennox had just checked her teeth for lipstick when Gretchen threw herself against the front door, barking hysterically. Shawn climbed the porch steps and stood on her porch, waiting for Lennox to get her dog under control. Lennox hooked her hand inside Gretchen's collar and tried to pull her back. "He's our friend, girl," Lennox said. But Gretchen wasn't having it. Her hackles rose, her lips curled, a deep growl rumbled in her chest. She weighed nearly as much as Lennox and wasn't wearing high heels.

Shawn threw his hands up in surrender and backed down the porch steps. Okay then…the good news was the Jagodas would think twice before they tried breaking into her house. The bad news was that Gretchen wasn't thrilled with Shawn. Lennox looked out her window and watched him climb into his car. She locked the house and clattered down the driveway to Shawn's car.

In the streetlight, trees cast forked shadows across the sidewalk. It was a rare clear night without wind. Even in the bright city, Lennox spotted Orion clearing the eastern horizon. She peeked through the car window at Shawn. It was hard to read much. "I'm so very sorry," she said before she'd completely opened the door.

"You didn't tell me you had an attack dog," he said before she'd closed it. He gave her a minute to settle in, then did a U-turn and headed west towards downtown. He was pissed, most definitely, looking straight ahead through the windshield, not even glancing at her. So she explained to the windshield how she'd never had a dog before, wasn't a pet person. "I'm working on Tomek Jagoda's case, and Tomek's family is bullying me. Breaking into my house, threatening me."

"Threatening you how?" Shawn said. And glanced at her.

"Besides breaking into my house twice, there's been some knife brandishing."

Shawn's irritation evaporated. "You should put in a good alarm system," he said. And, "I see you've installed bars and a security door. You need to make sure you have bars on all your windows including the basement."

In the spirit of trying to make a good date out of a bad start, Lennox pretended that she hadn't thought of that. They drove to the Portland Art Museum.

Shawn found a parking space seven blocks from their destination. By the time she made it up the steps of the place, her feet were killing her. Pitch a foot at a seventy-degree angle with nowhere to go but a pointed toe and convince her that wearing heels wasn't torture. She clung to Shawn's arm like a teenager in love for the first time.

Ten-foot silhouettes of witches and Halloween cats were backlit from the museum windows. The lobby twinkled from orange globes on the high-topped cocktail tables. Large glass pumpkins squatted in the corners.

"I'm sorry I'm grabbing you," she told Shawn at the coat check. "My feet are killing me."

"Sure," he said. And leaned closer to her. "Don't fight it, it's bigger than both of us." She pinched his arm and grinned. Maybe he'd forgiven her. Maybe they could have a good time after all.

The coat check guy gave them a number and told them to help themselves to an eye mask. Plain black satin for the guys, sequined ones for the women. Lennox tried on a black and gold sequined job, yanking on her hair so that it didn't pooch around the elastic band.

"You look smoking hot," Shawn said. "That dress." He shook his head like she'd nailed it.

She thanked him and told him he looked great, too. An old guy on a Steinway played show tunes: *Cats, Phantom of the Opera, Chicago.* She had to admit it was pretty fun getting dressed up and looking hot with a cute guy on her arm. And it was damned uncomfortable keeping her belly sucked in, with her toes feeling like someone was biting them. If she was at a normal party she'd kick off her shoes and go barefoot, but not with this crowd.

"Let's find the bar," she said.

Behind the bar hung a painting of a bunch of water lilies. Thirty people were already there, and more came through the doors, all in designer clothes, more than half the men in tuxes. Some folks brought their own masks: men with crazy bird of paradise masks in blue and green feathers or Venetian carnival masks. Mouths, that's all a person could see because the mask hid all the little muscles around their eyes. The whole anonymous thing was making people bolder, making *her* bolder. "I feel like we're headed for an orgy," Lennox said.

"Yeah?" Shawn said, and leaned closer. He smelled like dry cleaning fluid, but damn, he was good-looking. She drank a glass of champagne.

There, like an oasis in the desert, stood a bench in front of a fifteen-foot sculpture of a tortured spine. Oh man, to sit down! They claimed the bench, Lennox easing the heels from the back of her feet to give her toes breathing room. She sent Shawn for more bubbly while she scanned the room for someone among the masked partygoers she could still recognize.

Two judges were at the coat check and old man Bowersox, senior partner at Kline's firm, was sweeping a flute of champagne from the waitress's tray. Lennox recognized Portland's chief of police. Standing six-foot-seven, he was easy to spot. The chief laughed at his companion's joke. The companion was a short, stubby man with gray curls. Even with the mask, she recognized Doc Slocum. The chief bent and asked the doc a question. Slocum nodded and smiled. Back and forth they went, talking and smiling. It was hard to get a bead on who was schmoozing who. Lennox didn't know the chief personally. The mayor had appointed him after Lennox had been booted off the force. Still, the fact that they were so chummy pointed to a reason why Slocum had never become a person of interest.

In the corner, Lennox spotted Kline in a tux and black satin mask, looking pretty damn sexy. His mouth was stretched in a big white-toothed smile. Delighted. Who made him smile like that? Next to him was an impossibly tall Viking, tight black knit dress hugging her lean, perfect body. Jill Rykoff. Lennox was no slouch, but she was short and she was the girl next door, not a goddess. Lennox's dark hair barely covered her ears. All of a sudden, Lennox didn't feel special in her little black dress and heels. It was like her first prom in high school when her date waited for her on the curb in his Karmann Ghia, so drunk she could've been wearing a grocery sack for all he cared.

Wait a minute. What difference did it make how she stacked up against the Viking?

"Here you go." Shawn was back and handing her a new glass of champagne. Lennox tipped her head back and downed the glass, champagne bubbles sliding down her throat and filling her sinuses. She pressed the cocktail napkin Shawn had handed her against her nose.

"We need to talk to our host," she said. She shoved her feet into her shoes and launched herself from the bench with Shawn's help. Handsome as he was, she needed to get out of this situation, quit clinging to him. It was embarrassing.

She tried to keep her balance on the marble floor as they crossed the room to the corner table. On the wall behind Kline and Rykoff hung a huge red rectangle that Lennox could've painted, easy. Kline looked like he was having a helluva time with the goddess. Maybe there was nothing unethical about Kline talking to Jill, but it was bad form. He knew better.

Not that Lennox was Little Miss Ethics. She needed to get a serious grip. She was beautiful; she knew she was. And she was with a lovely guy who appreciated her, who jumped at any chance to see her. What was her fucking problem?

"Is that you, Cooper? You look great," Kline said. But not great enough to be called by her first name. "And this is?" he asked.

Lennox introduced Shawn to Kline.

Jill slid a sapphire blue mask over her perfect forehead. "Hi, it's me," she said, as if the room was filled with six-foot-tall Valkyrie. Jill shook hands with Lennox, then with Shawn. To give him credit, he handled the introduction without falling all over himself. A waiter appeared out of nowhere with a tray of champagne flutes. They each took one.

Jill slid the mask back in place and asked Shawn what he did for a living. She talked shop, laughed at his jokes. Kline laughed, too. Since when was he interested in patrol cops? Lennox's feet were killing her.

Lennox sipped her champagne. It didn't lessen her pain, but it did help her feel more detached. They made small talk. Jill was interested in Lennox's investigation of Hadley's murder. Of course she was.

"How is Gretchen?" Kline said.

"She's great," Lennox said. "We're bonding."

"She hates me," Shawn said. "Don't get me wrong. Under the circumstances—" He let the rest of the sentence dangle.

Lennox took his hand and squeezed it, hoping he got what she meant. Shut up. He was a cop, for godssake.

"What circumstances?" Jill plucked a dog hair from Lennox's dress and smiled, her tone conversational.

"You know," Shawn said. "The Jagodas."

Lennox could've kicked him. What kind of an Irishman was this guy that three glasses of champagne would make him so careless? Lennox glanced at Kline, who didn't seem to mind. Granted, he had a mask on, but still, he seemed oblivious to the fact that the case was being discussed and he and Jill were on opposite sides of the bench.

"The Jagodas are giving you trouble?" Jill said. Innocent as a lamb.

Before Shawn could speak up, Lennox said, "Yeah, Pieter and Idzi Jagoda. Why was there nothing in discovery about them?"

Kline seemed to wake up and look to Jill for an answer.

"They're in discovery as context."

Kline seemed satisfied with Jill's answer. Lennox was not. Why had Jill ignored Idzi and Pieter as possible suspects? Lennox finished her champagne and announced that she had an early morning interview.

"About the case?" Jill said, and then grinned. Her grin was followed by a grin from Kline, then Shawn. Last of all came Lennox, her smile too stiff to be called genuine.

"C'mon," she told Shawn and marched towards the cloak room, spine erect, without a wobble. She was getting the hang of this girl stuff. Grow ten inches and bleach her hair, she could be Jill.

"She was nice," Shawn said.

He was an idiot. A cute-as-hell idiot. And this was their third date: time for Shawn to make his move. They drove across the river before he asked her, "Would you like to come to my place? We could have a drink?"

She touched his arm. "I'm sorry. I'd love to, but I have to let Gretchen out, and you know..." she said.

She glanced at him. His profile downcast. This was a guy who was very polite and not accustomed to being turned down. He took a left at Alder and headed across the bridge to her house.

Gretchen was right. He was not the guy for her.

CHAPTER 17

That horseshit Jill had been spouting about Idzi and Pieter providing context in the Jagoda trial was not in discovery at all. And what about Slocum? Lennox spent the whole day combing through discovery for the hundredth time. Why had the cops zeroed in on Tomek and ignored Ito, Slocum, Idzi and Pieter? And what about Terry Purcell? It seemed to Lennox that Dick the dick gave up trying to find Terry too quickly.

Fog had set in by the time Lennox locked her office at five. A homeless guy crossed the street, pushing his grocery cart down the sidewalk in search of shelter for the night. Lennox headed home, picking up Halloween candy and a roasted chicken on the way. She heard Gretchen barking over the truck engine as she pulled into the driveway. Gretchen met her at the door with a big dog grin, her tongue hanging out, her whole behind wiggling in joy. Dogs! They were worth the shedding and the piles of excrement that needed bagging up, just for the shine of adoration that lit their big brown eyes. Lovers can fulfill a lot of needs, but no human can equal a dog's welcome home. It was the difference between disarming an alarm system and having somebody waiting for you to open the door.

Kline had come over last weekend and installed a dog gate between her kitchen and dining room and another one from her hallway to the living room to keep Gretchen from her front door. Then he'd stayed for a glass of wine. They sat on the sofa together, talking about the case, Gretchen stretched between them. The dog fell asleep, her paws twitching in a dream. It was cozy and there was no fire in the fireplace or candlelight or any of that shit.

Lennox pulled lettuce and carrots out of the fridge to make a salad to go with the chicken. And called Kline. "Can I give her some of my chicken?" Lennox asked him. "What about bones? Don't dogs love chewing on bones?"

Kline told her yes to the chicken, no to the bones. "Choking hazard," he said. She thanked him. Wished him a happy Halloween.

"Do you want to come over, hang with Gretchen, look at all the cute costumes?" she said. Purely spur-of-the-moment, no agenda.

There was a pause. An uncomfortable pause that made her guts clench. Goddamn! Did he think she was asking him out?

Was she?

"I'm sorry, I've got plans," he said.

Of course he did. Was his voice regretful? Embarrassed?

Lennox fell all over herself trying to exit the conversation, only making it worse. By then Gretchen was scratching at the back door. A week had gone by since Gretchen's arrival, and all Lennox's doors had claw marks. The doorbell rang. The first of the trick-or-treaters. Gretchen barked and charged the gate.

"Settle," she said, per Kline's instruction. Then she straddled the high gate and dished candy to a cute little toddler in a dinosaur costume.

Wine. She needed wine.

Hour after hour, the doorbell rang with costumed children to babies to mid-teens, a chorus of trick-or-treat, the fog pushed back from her porch by the light and the fire she'd managed to build between the demands of the doorbell. Gretchen got used to all the fuss and fell asleep on the kitchen rug. At eight-thirty, Lennox noticed a tall man standing behind the Felsteins' station wagon across the street. He was dressed in a black cloak with a giant hood that hid the top of a skull mask. He held a large scythe. The Grim Reaper. Was he a dad who hung back keeping tabs on his kids? More than one child had their parents dress in costume, but it was odd to shepherd your little ones around dressed as Death.

By nine o'clock, the younger kids had gone home. The doorbell was rung every fifteen minutes or so by high-schoolers. The Reaper had shifted closer, but he hung in the shadows of her neighbor's house. At nine thirty the Reaper was still there. He shifted from parked cars to her neighbors' yards, but always he seemed to be peering at Lennox. She locked the security door and turned off her porch light. Just as she turned the key, footsteps thumped up her porch steps. The Reaper stood at her door, staring at her behind his Death mask. Fear shot through all the cracks in her training as a cop. She backed from the door. Gretchen barked hysterically. Lennox unhinged the dog gate and Gretchen hurled herself against the front door, ropes of spit whipping from her bared lips.

The Reaper retreated into the fog. He must have parked some distance from her house. She didn't see or hear him drive away. She pulled the drapes, turned off the lights. Armed herself before she let Gretchen out back to do her business. Ham's voice was running through her head: *What's the matter with you, you should be carrying twenty-four seven.* What if she'd pulled a gun on Death? Then who would've been scared?

What *was* the matter with her? Everything, apparently.

The doorbell rang as Lennox relocked the back door. She didn't answer it. Didn't wash her face or brush her teeth. Screw it. She climbed the stairs to her bedroom, Gretchen galloping after her. Lennox tossed and turned trying to get comfortable before Gretchen leaped on her bed, all hundred pounds of her. The dog finally settled against Lennox's body and within moments was snoring. The fear that lodged in Lennox's throat began to dissolve and she was able to fall asleep.

Lennox was deeply asleep when the doorbell started ringing without a break. Pounding on the door. Gretchen leapt off the bed and ran down the stairs, barking all the way. The doorbell stopped its caterwaul.

"Jeffrey!" a woman's voice screamed. "I know you're in there. Fuck you, Jeffrey!" She pressed the doorbell again. Cathy Dunlap.

The screaming, the doorbell, and the dog barking was enough to make Lennox crazy. "Quiet," she shouted over the din. Her neighbors! What would her neighbors think? Another drama. Lennox was the only person on the block with this level of drama. Wasn't this exactly why Lennox paid all that rent to have an office, so she wouldn't have nut jobs coming to her house? No matter how hard Lennox worked, nothing changed.

Cathy pounded on the door. "Where is he?" she screamed.

Gretchen barked furiously.

Hard to think. Hard to talk.

Lennox told Gretchen to quiet, for all the good that did. She yelled through the door. "Calm down. He's not here. He's never been here."

"You're fucking him, I know you are. Come out here, Jeffrey!" She rattled the security door, which escalated the barking.

The woman was insane. Had Ito left her? Hard to blame him if he had. Lennox twitched the velvet curtains in the dining room for a view of the porch. Cathy stood under the porch light, her face pinched and red. She reached in the pocket of her work-out jacket. And drew out a pistol.

"Come out here," she yelled. "You have to face me."

Good God! Cathy was ready to shoot him. Or shoot her. Lennox grabbed Gretchen by the collar and dove to the corner between the dining room and the front door, away from all the windows. And dialed 911. Told the responder she had a woman on her porch waving a gun and making threats.

"I've called the police," Lennox yelled.

She heard Cathy sob and scream. "I hate you!" She kicked at the security door. The crack of gunshot. A bullet hitting metal.

The window behind the bars shivered, but held. Over the dog's barking, a car roared and sped away. Lennox peeked behind her curtains again and saw all the lights on at the Kurtzes' and the Felsteins'. Lennox decided to wait for the cops in case the Reaper was still out there somewhere.

Five minutes later the cops rang her doorbell. Gretchen went hysterical. Lennox dragged her into Fulin's room and closed the door.

Shawn Boyle stood beneath the porch light in his uniform. She unlocked the doors. He wore a professional, defender-of-the-good expression. Blue and red lights strobed across her neighbors' yards. Anybody asleep during Cathy's tirade was sure to be awake now. Shawn's partner looked like Shawn had briefed him about Lennox. His name was Elijah. He was black and looked too young to be a cop.

Gretchen slammed herself against Fulin's door.

"Is the dog secured?" Shawn asked, the tip of his nose red from the cold, his gun hand hovering over his belt.

"Yes."

"Other than the dog, you're alone?" Shawn said.

Yes. She let them in. Gretchen clawed Fulin's door. Lennox's head was pounding from exhaustion and adrenaline.

"The woman who pulled a gun on me is Cathy Dunlap," she said. She gave Shawn Cathy's address. "I don't know what kind of gun it was, exactly. Some kind of lady gun. I saw her pull it out of her pocket and I ducked."

Shawn's partner looked up from his notebook. "Did she ring the doorbell, then pull a gun on you?"

"She wanted in my house. She thought I was harboring her boyfriend."

"Were you?" Shawn said, his face looking afraid of what she'd say.

"Of course not," Lennox said.

"The boyfriend's name?" Elijah said.

Lennox explained the whole deal.

Shawn and Elijah searched the front of her house with flashlights and found where Cathy had hit the security bars on Lennox's dining room window. They looked for the slug. Eventually they found it in the bark dust beneath an overgrown camellia by the corner of her house.

It was past one in the morning. Her body sagged with fatigue. They'd taken her statement and asked her if she wanted to press charges. "Absolutely," she told them. It was about time to give her trouble some trouble. She thanked the guys for showing up.

Shawn hung back as Lennox shut the door. "Do you want to go to dinner, maybe Sunday?" He smiled wide and hopeful.

She told him how nice that would be, but she was stretched to the limit on Tomek's case.

"I guess it doesn't matter whether he's guilty or not, so long as you get paid," Shawn said.

That was a shit thing to say, and she told him so.

He looked at her like he couldn't figure her out. It was simple, really. Life was no longer good versus evil. She'd become a PI, someone who had more in common with defense attorneys than cops. Shawn turned and climbed down the steps to the waiting patrol car and lifted a hand in farewell. "Later," he said.

Lennox locked the door behind him. She phoned Ito and got his voicemail. She told him it was urgent. Cathy was out looking for him, and she had a gun. "Call me," she said.

She made herself a cup of tea and waited for Jeff to call back. Gretchen, worn out from all the guard duty, watched Lennox pace the living room for fifteen minutes, a half hour. She called him again and left him a second voicemail.

Fucking guy, where was he? Probably out getting high. And Cathy was roaming the city looking for him, driven crazy by suspicion and disappointment. Cathy was over forty, she should've known she couldn't remake Jeff into her ideal man. It was wrong-headed.

It was going on two o'clock. When was enough enough?

"C'mon Gretchen," Lennox said. "Let's go to bed."

CHAPTER 18

Lennox had reached Jeff Ito at seven the following morning. "Did you get my messages from last night?" she'd asked. He mumbled something. Why did she make any effort at all with this guy? He deserved to get shot. They agreed to meet at her office. She gave him the address.

Lennox drank her Americano as she waited for him. The wind blasted against her office windows. Leaves and the trash from homeless people who'd camped in doorways in the neighborhood clattered down the street. The building began to fill up, the acupuncturist already open for business. Cowboy boots clicked past her door, and the architect unlocked his office further down the hall.

Jeff called on the intercom at nine sharp and she buzzed him in. He looked freshly scrubbed and wore a crisp shirt, but it didn't hide the sag of skin under his eyes and chin. He was hungover.

She asked him to sit down.

"Is Cathy in jail?" he said.

"I'm not sure. Have you tried calling her?"

He smiled nervously. "I thought I'd talk to you first."

Lennox loved it. The guy had barely sat down, and she smelled the powerful scent of evidence. It smelled like fear with a top note of self-preservation. She pulled her notebook from the center desk drawer.

"Why was Cathy looking for you at my house?" she said.

"Your address is on your business card."

"Yeah, fine, but that's not what I'm asking."

"You're really good-looking." Jeff shifted his weight in the chair, looked around the room. Then he shrugged. "Maybe she thought you and I were seeing each other or something."

"You and me?" She was baffled. "Why would she think that?"

Jeff looked at the floor. "Cathy asked me if I'd met with you yet, and I said no."

Lennox set her pen down on the desk. Jeff was worse than the homeless dude she interviewed on the library lawn. She stopped breathing when she heard this kind of horseshit. She inhaled. "Do you lie for a reason or is it just recreational?"

"You've met her, you know how jealous she is. Used to be she was sweet. She trusted me. Then she started to see this crazy psychic. Now she and her pal are going twice a week at a hundred and fifty bucks a pop." A vein pulsed near Jeff's temple. He looked flushed and genuinely pissed off, which made what he said seem more credible than most of the nonsense he spouted. "We're supposed to be saving for our honeymoon," he said. "Not that that's going to happen. The psychic says don't trust me. It's all in the cards. The tower. The five of something. The psychic says that I'm cheating on her. That I'm unreliable."

He looked at Lennox like he was waiting for her to reassure him. Instead she asked him for the pal's name. Abby Slocum.

"Any relation to Dr. Jim Slocum?"

"She's his wife. You think Cathy's bad, that one's a real piece of work."

Did Jeff know Dr. Slocum?

No.

"Because Hadley called Dr. Slocum the night of her murder," Lennox said. "And Cathy knew his wife."

"I don't know him. Okay?" Jeff said. "I never knew half the shit Hadley was up to, and as for Abby, she's a stuck-up princess."

For once, Lennox felt sure Ito was telling the truth. She asked for the psychic's name.

Mrs. Tamer.

"How long has the psychic been telling Cathy that you're not Mr. Right?"

He chewed his lower lip as he thought. "Maybe a month before the Hadley thing happened."

"You mean the Hadley being murdered thing?"

He looked down at her desk and then up at her. Just wait until Kline got a hold of this guy on the stand. He'd have him for lunch.

"Cathy woke up at six that morning after Hadley was killed," she said. "You had already left."

He ran his hand across his mouth. Had he not thought it all the way through? Was it possible that he hadn't realized that now that he'd made enemies with Cathy, both their alibis were useless?

"It's not what you think," he said.

"What do I think?"

He took a beat to study her face. "That I waited for Cathy to fall asleep, then went to party with Hadley."

"It's plausible." She shrugged.

"It wasn't like that. Cathy was restless, tossing and turning. Then when she finally fell asleep, she started snoring," he said. "Look, I didn't do anything wrong. Hadley was dead when I got there."

"What time?"

"Maybe four?" he said. He watched her reaction. "Maybe I should get a lawyer?"

"Maybe you should," she said. "I got to say your alibi looks null at this point."

He looked like she'd slapped him. "It wasn't what you think. I came home. The front door was open, CDs all over the floor, furnace running non-stop. I didn't look at the clock. Okay? I'm trying to cooperate here."

Mr. Cooperation was running scared. The lawyer was off the table for now.

"So you arrived maybe four? Hadley doing the dead man's float in your tub?"

"Yeah, that's exactly how it was," he said. He sounded more confident.

"The police clocked the call from you at six," she said. "You did what between four and six?"

"I was in shock," he swallowed. "I cared about her."

"You found her floating face down in your tub. So she was floating on the top?" Would he answer the question the way he answered the cops? (Top.) The way he answered her at the Heathman? (Top. Bottom. He couldn't remember.)

"I only saw she was drowned. I don't remember where in the tub. It was terrible. My first dead person and it was Hadley." He stood up.

"One more question. Sit down," she said.

He hesitated.

"Sit," she said.

He sat.

"So no alibi," she said.

She threw him a life jacket. "Could Cathy somehow have made it to your house before you did?" It was truly gorgeous the range of emotions that passed across his face: hope and guile being the chief things she recognized. He was willing to betray his fiancée. It was good for the case, bad for Lennox's general regard for humanity.

"I went to the bar after I left Cathy's," he said. "She could've gone to my house before I did."

"What bar?"

"I don't know. Just a bar."

"C'mon Jeff."

"It was one of those bars in a strip mall on the way home," he said. "Lucky Larry's?"

She took a deep breath. "When you turn your answers into questions, it's hard to believe one fucking word that comes out of your mouth."

The profanity seemed to focus him. "Lucky Larry's." A definite answer.

"This time I want the truth. Not what you think will absolve you of guilt. The truth. When did you leave Cathy's?"

"Two o'clock," he said. The lying sack of shit.

She threw her notebook in the drawer and slammed it shut. "The bars close at two o'clock," she said. "Go home."

He leaned forward. "Okay," he said. "Okay. I'll tell you. I got to the bar just after one o'clock. My friend was working. She locked up after closing and we had a few more drinks. I got to my house at four, like I said. That's the truth. I just didn't want my friend to get in trouble."

The bartender was a woman. The psychic had been right about him. "Will your friend back your story?" she said.

"Yeah, but see, her boss doesn't like after-hours parties."

Lennox watched him try to sell this version of his story. She remembered when she'd first met Jeff and thought he was handsome in a bad boy sort of way. Now she couldn't look at him without wanting to beat the crap out of him. She'd known some real liars over the years. Hell, what was poker if it wasn't trying to bluff the other guy. She took some deep cleansing breaths, retrieved her notebook, and wrote down the friend's name and phone number.

"One more time," she said. She tapped the notebook with her pen. Kline could discredit Ito's testimony on the witness stand, but that didn't get Lennox any closer to whether Jeff or his girlfriend or someone else did the crime.

"You did what from four to six when you called the cops?" She braced herself for how he was going to spin this.

"Okay." He rubbed the corner of his mouth with a finger. "Okay. So, Hadley had a bottle of Oxys in her purse and I was in shock, you know? I never meant to, but I'd been drinking. I guess I passed out."

CHAPTER 19

Was Cathy Dunlap a little controlling, but still sane person until the psychic turned her into a raving psycho bitch? Who was this Mrs. Tamer and what kind of a name is that for a psychic? Shouldn't her name be Madame X, or something? There wasn't much that Lennox could find in the records. Tamer's first name was Theodora, and she was fifty-five years old and widowed from her second husband five years ago. There was no mortgage on her million-dollar house; she had no debts and a credit card she hardly used. She appeared to be operating on a mostly cash basis, like a drug dealer. She'd had a number of expensive speeding tickets over the years, otherwise no record of wrong-doing.

Mrs. Tamer lived in a mock Tudor in the posh neighborhood of Laurelhurst. The trees were large and old, the houses large and old as well. The woman who opened the door was very different from what Lennox expected. She wasn't wearing a purple cape or a pointy hat or anything like that. She had a tiny child's body and doe eyes, her abundant hennaed hair held away from her skull with a big alligator clip. From a distance, Lennox would've pegged her age somewhere in her twenties, but up close her face and neck were webbed with wrinkles. Lennox wondered about her health. Tamer wore a long sweater that hung to her knees, leggings that encased her stick legs.

Mrs. Tamer's eyes opened even wider. "Officer?"

"Cooper," Lennox said. She must've picked up on Lennox's cop vibe. Still, shouldn't she have intuited that Lennox was at present in the private sector? "May I have a word?"

Mrs. Tamer moved aside to let Lennox enter. "I'm sorry for your loss."

"Excuse me?" Lennox said.

"Grief is pouring off you." Then she grabbed Lennox's hand. They were still on a small patch of tile inside the doorway. "This recent tragedy will scar over and you'll know more joy than you've experienced up until now."

Lennox wasn't keen on strangers touching her or offering her comfort about something they didn't have any damn business knowing about. But she followed the psychic through the darkened living room where an ancient woman slept in front of a golf game on the television. On the far wall, incense smoke threaded into the air in front of a five-foot-tall goddess statue. The room seemed saturated with the sweet smoke. Mrs. Tamer led Lennox down a wide tiled hallway to a sunroom. Even though the morning was overcast, large windows filled the room with a gray light.

Mrs. Tamer lit a candle and closed her eyes. Her ringed fingers twitched in the trance or whatever it was. She stayed that way: eyes closed, fingers twitching. Lennox glanced at her watch. More time passed. Lennox took in the wallpaper pattern (pale peach roses on a silvery background) and breathed the incense laden air.

Finally Tamer opened her eyes and lifted a deck of cards from a small wooden box. How Lennox loved a deck of cards. These were different, though, larger than an ordinary deck. When the tiny psychic shuffled them, they didn't have the crisp snap that Lennox loved. These cards were well-used. After the shuffle, Mrs. Tamer placed the cards on the table.

Lennox resisted the urge to turn one over. She tore her eyes away from the deck. "I'm investigating the murder of Hadley Eberhart."

"I know," Mrs. Tamer said. "But first cut the deck." Her expression was neutral. This woman had Cathy Dunlap in her thrall, along with who knew how many other people.

"Don't be afraid," Mrs. Tamer said, like a dare. A sliver of a smile tugged the edges of Tamer's lipsticked mouth.

"Of cards?" Lennox cut the deck. They were limp with age and warm to the touch. The psychic nodded in satisfaction and placed the first card on the table facing Lennox.

"See?" Mrs. Tamer said. "The Nine of Wands."

The card showed a wounded man in an orange tunic leaning on a staff, a large bandage covering most of his hair. Lennox saw herself staring in the bathroom mirror a year ago, the day she got home from the hospital. The day she unwound the bandage from her head and shaved her scalp. Fulin was dead and life would never be the same again.

She shivered. And hated herself for shivering. Mrs. Tamer watched her intently. Of course she did. This was her business.

The psychic poked the card with a bony finger. "The

defense card. See his expression? He's wary. The problem isn't over yet."

"You have a client," Lennox said. "Cathy Dunlap. She's been seeing you a lot lately."

"That's privileged information," Tamer said.

Lennox could've argued with her about legalities, how psychics don't have immunity like priests and lawyers do. Instead, Lennox appealed to Tamer's better nature. "I'm trying to help a mentally disabled man who's been charged with murder."

Tamer's face hardened into a mask. Even though Lennox was a poker player and a detective, she couldn't read her. Tamer lifted the next card off the deck and placed it across the bandaged head. King of Swords. He was seated, dressed in a blue robe, his expression resolute. He was handsome, judgmental. "This card is in the position of helps or hindrances. He's a professional man. A doctor, maybe, or an attorney."

Kline. Both a help and a hindrance, this woman was spooking her out. "You advised Cathy that Jeff was a cheat," Lennox said.

"He is a cheat," the psychic said. "The past." Tamer was more intent than any poker player waiting for the river card. But unlike Texas Hold'em, this card didn't fill a potential straight. Clouds, rain, a red heart pierced through by three swords. "I knew it. Grief," Mrs. Tamer said. Did she see Fulin's death? Know that Lennox could never really recover? "There is a silver lining in all this sadness," she said. "Because spiritual growth only occurs from necessary elimination."

Fulin a necessary elimination? The muscle beneath Lennox's eye began to tick, and the psychic saw it, knew she was getting to Lennox.

"Bullshit," Lennox said. She wanted to grab the woman by the throat and shake her. Instead she shoved the cards towards the psychic. Lennox knew that you don't interfere with a deal.

Mrs. Tamer gasped as Lennox knew she would. Now who was psychic?

"You don't believe in Spirit," Tamer said.

"Cathy has become erratic," Lennox said. "You have observant powers, you must have noticed. Did you realize that she had a gun? Used it?"

"You're not a policewoman. You used to be, but now you're a private detective."

"Common knowledge," Lennox said. "At one time you told Cathy that marriage and a happy family were in her future. Lately though, you've been forecasting betrayal. Is it possible Cathy could've killed someone to protect her family?"

"You're the woman who's having an affair with Jeff Ito."

"Wrong," Lennox said. "He's someone I'm investigating."

She nodded. "That makes sense," she said. "What I sensed was an intimacy. It could be your inquiry."

Mrs. Tamer placed the three cards in the same constellation as before—bandaged head, Kline crossed, heart pierced with three swords. "Recent event," Mrs. Tamer said, and laid a fourth card to the left of Kline. "Three of Wands reversed. Spreading yourself too thin. Lack of cooperation."

"Jeff Ito tells me that Cathy is seeing you twice a week at $150 a crack. When it was marriage and happiness, she was content to see you once a month."

"Jeff's not a suitable husband for Cathy," Mrs. Tamer said.

"How do you know that? You've never met him."

"The cards. Infidelity. Two of queens, three of cups reversed. It indicates drugs, alcohol, sex. Jeff and his old girlfriend still went to parties where they drank and drugged after he moved in with Cathy," the psychic said.

"How do you know that?" Lennox said. "You couldn't possibly know that."

"Cathy knows that. It's in her subconscious. Her conscious mind can't admit the knowing. That's how the cards work."

"Was it just Cathy's subconscious, or had she looked for proof of Jeff's infidelity after you raised suspicion?"

"Wouldn't anyone look for proof? Cathy has a lot at stake. She has a young child she's responsible for."

"And did she find proof?"

"Let's turn back to you," Tamer said.

The psychic turned another card over. Another card and another card. Clubs, swords. Strife. Effort. "Ah," she said. "Finally the major arcana. Justice." A woman draped in red and crowned in gold holding a sword in her right hand and the scales in her left.

Of course.

"Final outcome?" Mrs. Tamer said. Her hand hovered over the deck.

Final outcome. Fulin gone. Kline and Jill. The future.

Mrs. Tamer lifted her eyes from the deck and trained them on Lennox's face the way a poker player would study an opponent for tells. She turned the card over.

"Ten of Cups," she said.

A man and wife, their arms encircling each other's waist. The landscape is theirs: woods, house, hills. The whole thing painted in pastel colors. Two children skipping merrily in the foreground, a rainbow overhead. Lennox could feel herself being watched.

This woman was seriously fucking with her. Lennox could bounce out of there, or she could learn something. "You win," she said. "You've got my number."

Lennox pointed to the Justice card. "What do the cards say? Who killed Hadley Eberhart?"

The psychic laid her hand on the deck, her eyes unfocused for a moment. Then she nodded. "Cut the cards," she said.

Was it her imagination or were the cards even warmer this time?

Mrs. Tamer turned the top card and laid it on top of Justice. "Page of swords reversed. You know the murderer."

CHAPTER 20

It was nine at night. Fog pressed against Lennox's windows. Now that Gretchen was living with Lennox, Kline had taken to meeting at Lennox's place and Lennox had taken to stocking Kline's scotch.

After they settled in, Gretchen leapt next to her on the sofa, turned in a tight circle three times, and then flopped against her with a grunt.

"The two of you seem to be getting along," Kline said.

Lennox patted Gretchen's flank, traced her red eyebrows with a finger. Daddy, Mommy, and baby bear. The three of them sat companionably for a few minutes. This was how families were together. Maybe. Not like her folks Al and Aurora and Baby Lennox.

"It's nice here." Kline pointed a toe towards the fireplace. Lennox had wondered if building a fire was sending the wrong message. Like she was trying to make their having a drink together and talking about the case romantic or something. When did she start overthinking every stupid thing?

Kline broke the silence to ask her what she had for him.

"Ito," she said. And re-focused. "Mostly Ito and his girlfriend. I interviewed Jeff again. You'd have a field day with this guy. His alibi is a bunch of hooey, which means hers is as well. He can't remember if he left the house at one, two or four. He finally landed on one o'clock. His newest alibi is a lady bartender at Lucky Larry's."

"A drinking man's alibi." Kline tapped his pencil against the legal pad. "You've talked to the bartender?"

"Chelsea Bennett. She verified she'd seen Jeff on the night of October 9, but when I asked her what day of the week that was, she was unclear. Turned out Ito stayed after hours one night maybe two, three weeks ago, maybe a month, she didn't remember. But say he was there the night of October 9, that still leaves Cathy Dunlap. Believe me, that woman would've drowned Hadley in a heartbeat."

"So tell me the story," he said.

"Starting with Ito. There were plenty of reasons to be mad at Hadley. Chiefly because she got him in dutch with Cathy, calling him and begging for money."

Kline swallowed a mouthful of scotch and jotted notes, his pencil scratching across a legal pad. The fire found a pocket of pitch and snapped.

"He drove home from the bar," she continued. "Having consumed four drinks according to Chelsea. Found Hadley loaded and naked in his hot tub. She had trashed the living room, found his secret hidey hole for vodka. He was fed up with her, he'd never get her out of his life, so he drowned her."

"His motive for murder is he's fed up?" Kline shook his head in disbelief. "That's weak."

"What about jealousy?"

Lennox elaborated how Cathy had gone from loving fiancée to shoot 'em up crazy lady.

"She shot your house?" Kline set down his scotch. His ears went bright red. "With Gretchen here?"

The way he leaned on Gretchen's name, she wondered who he was more concerned about. She asked him.

"Both of you. Of course. I just don't know why these things keep happening to you."

"Because I'm a detective," Lennox said.

Kline put his head in his hands, his elbows braced on his knees. "I don't know," he finally said. "It wasn't like this when I worked with Calderbank."

"Like what?" she said. She was pissed at Kline for throwing another investigative agency in her face.

"The danger," he said.

"That's because they're a big corporate company. I'll bet you never met the real people who did the work."

Besides Jeff and Cathy, Lennox told him about Hadley's doctor, who handed out prescriptions for speed and opiates like he was handing out Halloween candy. Possible motive was blackmail. "And that's not even including Idzi or Pieter," she said. "Motive: Theft of product."

Kline had quit taking notes. He tapped his pencil against the legal pad.

"Rykoff's offered a plea bargain," he said.

Rykoff. Fucking Rykoff. And Kline was willing to throw the case away. The night at the party, did he sleep with her?

"A plea bargain," she said. "Aw, isn't that sweet?"

Kline set the pad and pencil on the table and stared at her. What niceness remained after the Calderback crack went up in smoke. Gretchen jumped off the sofa and rubbed herself against Kline's leg. Mummy and Daddy were fighting. Were they ever.

"Why would she offer you a deal unless there's weakness somewhere in their case?" she said.

Okay, so he noticed that she'd sounded shrill. What was it about Jill and Kline that twisted her gut? Like she didn't know.

"She's offering Jagoda assault three," Kline said.

"You want to take that? He'd get ten years!"

"Face it, Lennox," he said. "Jagoda admitted he was there. He fled. He's a drug dealer. They found his fingerprint. Rubber gloves in his trash can."

"You know they can't use the gloves. Anyone could've put them in the dumpster."

"You have five suspects and no proof."

"He's innocent," Lennox said.

"Tell me about innocent," Kline said. "He's a drug dealer from a family of drug dealers."

"He did not kill Hadley Eberhart. I'm completely sure of it."

He shook his head.

"Gus, he can't make an important decision like that without counsel."

"I am his counsel," Kline said. "I think it's the best we can manage."

"You're going to urge Tomek to take a felony charge when he didn't do the crime?"

"And you know he didn't drown the librarian based on what? A feeling? Did he cry? Tell you he loved her?"

"You've never been a cop," she said. "You've got to trust your gut. Anyway, what's Tomek's motive? You tell me the story."

Kline shrugged. "Jealousy. He found her naked in her ex-boyfriend's hot tub."

"I've talked to both Tomek and Ito. They've never met. Didn't even know each other's names."

"Maybe they're both lying."

"Five credible suspects," she said. "Exploding alibis, an assault charge against one of them."

"No proof."

"Where's the prosecution's proof? It's all circumstantial. If they're holding out a deal for us, there's got to be a hole in their case," she said. "I've got a meeting with Tomek first thing tomorrow morning. He might have remembered something I can use."

"You combed over their discovery again and again and didn't come up with a thing."

"There was no mention of Idzi or Pieter. Why?"

"Context," he said.

"Those are Rykoff's words." Lennox had gone from loving his company to wanting to smack him.

He drained his scotch. "She's not going to hold out the deal indefinitely."

"Use your charm," Lennox said. For the first time, Cathy made sense. Lennox knew how you could care about a guy and want him to become something different.

Kline planted his empty glass on the end table and stood up. "You've got three days."

She locked the door behind him. That feeling of domestic contentment when he'd first come in? Gone. She trudged up the stairs to the bedroom, Gretchen loping behind her. Lennox unwrapped a new deck of tarot cards she'd picked up at the wu-wu bookstore down the street from her office. She spread the cards over her quilt—fear images of people fighting, crying, dead, The Moon, the nine of swords, The Tower. Then the six of cups: an older boy offering a golden-haired girl a huge flower-filled goblet. Why were the yellow-haired girls the ones that get the flowers?

She woke up shivering on top of the bed, the lights on, cards strewn across the quilt. Swords, Moon, Hanged Man. What was going to happen to Tomek? To her? Gretchen stretched out across the foot of the bed. She patted the dog who grunted but did not wake up. She gathered up the cards and turned off the light.

CHAPTER 21

Brass stalagmites flanked the steps leading to the Multnomah County Justice Center. The jail. The stalagmites were supposed to be art, but no one Lennox ever met thought they were beautiful or even interesting. The fog had lifted sometime during the night, replaced with a wind that blew from the south across hundreds of miles of a warmer Pacific Ocean. The air was so heavy with moisture that a body got damp without it ever raining. After Halloween, the days—even when it didn't rain—were more twilight than daylight.

Lennox climbed the granite steps leading to the jail, dumped her boots and briefcase in a brown plastic tub, and passed through security. Doris waved hello to Lennox from the security desk. Her silver crew cut matched the metallic wall behind her.

"Who are we bailing out this time?" Doris said.

"Not bailing out. Visiting," Lennox said. "Tomek Jagoda."

She asked Doris about her grandson while Doris typed

into the computer to verify that Lennox was on the visitors list. Doris asked about Lennox's love life.

"I got a dog," Lennox said.

You'd think Lennox was having a kid the way Doris gushed. Doris adored Rotties. "Those soulful eyes," she said. "The way they wiggle their behinds when they're happy." Doris second-checked the contents of Lennox's briefcase, riffled the pages of her notebook, ran her finger along the back of Lennox's photo arrays.

"Her head is almost as big as a microwave," Lennox said. "You should see what she's done to my backyard."

"But they're such good company," Doris said. She patted Lennox down. Made her take off her boots again.

It was true, Gretchen was good company. The dog followed Lennox down to the basement when she put a load in the washer, followed her into the kitchen when Lennox made a sandwich or a pot of coffee. Followed her to bed, her warm sleeping body snuggled up against Lennox at night.

"You're right," Lennox said. "I don't care if my backyard has become her toilet."

"I had to go with a Westie on account of I live in a condo."

Lennox nodded and smiled even though she had no idea what a Westie looked like or even for sure that it was a dog. The pneumatic locks hissed and released. Doris waved her through.

Tomek slumped at the Formica visiting table in the same dirty white interview room. He looked paler than the last time she saw him and smelled sour. Fear smelled sour. It could be that. It could be a lot of things: what he ate, whether his uniform was left in the washer overnight.

"How are they treating you?" she said.

"Okay." He stared at the table.

"You've had time to think," she said. "Who might've wanted to hurt Hadley?"

He shook his head. He still wasn't making eye contact.

Lennox reached into her briefcase and showed him photo arrays: one that included Jeff, one Cathy, one Dr. Slocum.

Tomek shook his head.

"Try," she said. "I need you to try to help me. You're the only one who can save yourself."

"Don't remember," he mumbled.

"Tell me about the house where you found Hadley. Had you been there before?"

His body slumped as if his strings were cut.

"When Hadley called you that night she gave you the address out in Cedar Hills. Didn't you ask her who lived way out there?"

No.

"Look at me, Tomek." She waved her hand in front of him, finally getting eye contact. "Who's going to help me if you don't?"

"I don't know what you mean," he said.

"I know five people who might've wanted to hurt Hadley. Do you think any one of them is going to tell me the bad things they've done?"

"I guess not." His eyes slid off hers and he took to looking at the table again.

"It's not just about getting you out of here," she said. "It's about making Hadley's killer pay for what he did."

That seemed to reach him. He nodded. "The cops told

me it was Jeff Ito's house where Hadley was. He was her ex-boyfriend."

"But you've never seen him?"

He shook his head.

"You didn't know his name before the cops told you?"

"I didn't know."

"You never sold him speedballs? Look at these photos again," she said. "Do any of them look familiar?"

He ran his thumb over each photo. The tip of his tongue poked out from the corner of his mouth. He looked up at her as if he'd failed a test.

"You told me before you never gave Hadley speedballs."

"She never took those."

"But you sell them, right? Your thumbprint was on a packet found at the crime scene. Do you know what that means, Tomek?"

He looked at Lennox, waiting for her to tell him.

"It could be a plant. One of your customers left the paper at the crime scene with your thumbprint to make the police believe you killed Hadley."

She waited a moment to give him time to think. Then had him look at the photo arrays again.

"Can you name anyone you sold speedballs to?" she said. She heard the desperation in her own voice. "Otherwise how did your thumbprint show up next to where Hadley was murdered?"

He shook his head.

"Think," she said.

He punched himself in the head, hard. Then again.

"Don't," she said. Christ! She'd pushed him too far. She grabbed his forearm.

The guard uncrossed his arms and strode towards the

table, his hand hovering over a Taser holstered on his belt. She let go of Tomek, told him to stop. Please stop.

"My fault," she told the guard. "I'm with Tomek's defense team. Give me just a minute. It's so important."

The guard narrowed his eyes, his hand still on the Taser.

She turned her notebook pages back to an early list. "Tomek, this is a list of people Hadley called the night of her murder. She called you twice. Here's your number, once at ten o'clock, another time at 11:30. She called a Dr. Slocum, she called Jeff Ito, she called Terry Purcell. Do any of those names ring a bell?"

"Hadley used to go out with Jeff Ito," he said. "The cops told me."

"That's right," she said. "There's Jeff Ito's name, your name. Any other name that looks familiar to you?"

"Terry Purcell," he said.

Terry Purcell didn't exist. Hadley had made a call to a burner phone. "Who is Terry Purcell?" she said. She clutched her pen so hard her knuckles turned white. This could be the break she'd been praying for.

"Some guy."

"Some guy you sell speedballs to?"

"Yeah," he said. "Sometimes. Sometimes cocaine."

A lead she could bring back to Kline, make another bid for his patience. She asked Tomek to describe Terry. He was tall, but not as tall as Tomek or his brother. And he was skinny. Gay.

"How do you know he's gay?" she said.

He shrugged. "Sometimes you know."

Fair enough. "Thank you," she said. "I know it has been painful for you to talk about this."

She took a deep breath. She told him to take one, too.

"We need to reset," she said. She watched him wait for her prompt. "Your lawyer's going to offer you a plea deal. Do you know what that is?"

"Kinda," he said.

"He's going to tell you to agree to assault three. That means you pushed Hadley under the water and watched her drown."

"No!" he said. He was finally there in the room with her.

"It means ten years in jail and a permanent record of a felony."

"No," he said. "No."

"That's what you need to tell Mr. Kline when he tries to talk you into accepting a felony assault. You did not touch Hadley in anger. Am I right?"

"Right," he said.

"Then tell him you're innocent of the crime. Tell him you won't settle."

• • •

Friday night. Lennox walked the mile to the Shanty to clear her mind. It had quit raining late in the afternoon, but the trees still showered water on her head and shoulders as she walked along Broadway.

Terry Purcell, a skinny gay guy that Hadley had called the night of her murder. A guy with a fake name using a burner phone. Lennox knew the murderer the psychic had said. Maybe. But why should she trust Mrs. Tamer for one minute? It didn't take a card shark to plant a card when you did an overhand shuffle the way Tamer did. But Tamer was one hundred percent right about Jeff Ito. And Lennox trusted her gut when it came to Tomek's innocence. How was that so different?

Tamer had pointed to Justice when she read Lennox's fortune. That's what Lennox wanted for the little librarian. Whoever it was that cut her life short should have to pay for it. How in hell was Lennox going to find the owner of a burner phone?

She pushed the Shanty's door open into a dim room full of damp cops. Three television screens lit with a football game. The bar was solid with patrolmen, a few shabbily dressed detectives scattered amongst them. Lennox spotted Sarge's shiny head two-thirds of the way down the bar gassing with a patrolman. If Sarge knew Lennox had not only seen a psychic, but was actually taking the woman seriously, he would give simultaneous birth to three cows.

She waved to him and continued to the back room.

Ham, Jerry, and 2-K were already seated around the stained green table, the guys trading cash for poker chips.

"It's our girl," Jerry said when she walked in, his face all warm and welcoming. He looked at her more closely. "Everything okay with you?"

Some things she couldn't share with the guys, some things they'd never understand. She glanced at the Clydesdales pulling a wagon of Budweiser on the wall over Jerry's head. "It's been a weird couple of days," she said.

"Every day is weird when you work with the public," he said.

Ham looked up at her from the stacks of bills and chips on the table.

"How's Shawn?"

"Not sure," she said. "We haven't talked recently."

"I thought you guys were a thing."

Sarge and Fish walked into the room. They hung their jackets on the pegs by the door. "A thing?" Fish said.

"Shawn Boyle."

"Don't tell me you ditched him, too," Fish said.

"We only went out a couple of times. It wasn't a big deal."

Ham sighed and started shuffling the cards.

"I don't get it," Fish said. "He's a great guy."

"Gretchen doesn't like him."

"You're letting a dog choose who you go out with?" Fish was incredulous.

"Not a bad idea," Jerry said. "Does the dog have to be a Rottweiler?"

Ham cleared his throat noisily. "Five card draw, jacks or better." He passed the cards to Sarge for the cut.

Lennox waited to look at her cards until everyone had picked up their hand. The peek was her rabbit's foot. It was how she courted Luck, if Luck could be courted. She didn't know if it worked or not, but a body's got to do something not to surrender to chaos. Her hand was two sixes, two threes, and the king of spades. Swords, spades, same thing. *A lawyer*, Mrs. Tamer had said. Kline.

Fish opened with a five-buck chip. Lennox threw in her chip. Everyone stayed in.

"Lennox?" Ham waited for her discard. She threw in the king and drew a five. She was left with two pair.

Sarge took the hand with three tens.

They played for two hours. Lennox was up fifty bucks. She'd heard Jerry's new stories about his neurotic but totally hot girlfriend. Sarge talked about his new boat.

It was Ham's deal again.

"Kline's given me three days to offer him something

148

substantive," she said. "Or he's going to counsel Jagoda to plead down."

"How far down?" Jerry said.

"Assault three," she said.

2-K blew the air out of his cheeks. "Ouch."

"Rykoff's going for D.A.," Jerry said. "She wouldn't take the case if it wasn't a sure deal."

Ham set the deck down and looked across the table at her. "Maybe it's for the best."

"Don't say that," she said. "Rykoff wouldn't have even offered Kline a plea bargain unless there was a weak spot somewhere in her case."

"Is there?" Sarge said.

"They have no proof. And you know what the prosecutor said when I asked her point blank why Idzi and Pieter Jagoda weren't mentioned in discovery? She said they were context. Nowhere does that show up."

"They're a crime family. That's the context," Fish said. "The vic was Tomek's girlfriend."

"They didn't even take her ex-boyfriend in for questioning," Lennox said. "The murder happened at his house, his alibi is crap, and he's a drug user."

"So you think the ex did the murder?" Fish said.

"I don't know," she admitted. Terry Purcell. The pill doctor.

"Rykoff's got the right guy," Fish said. "The whole family's bad news."

The guys, every one of them, even Ham, nodded their heads.

"You've got it wrong," she said. "Tomek's innocent."

Jerry looked around the table before he met her eyes.

His expression was not unkind. "Lennox, I'm sorry, but I got to say this. Jagoda's not Fulin. You can't save the world."

Lennox felt their eyes burning into her, felt the flush rise from her cheeks up to the roots of her hair. She dug in her bag for her wallet, pulled out two twenties, two fives. Stacked up her chips on top of the cash. "A hundred bucks says Tomek Jagoda goes free." She looked around the table. "Any takers?"

Jerry shook his head. Likewise Ham, 2-K and Sarge.

"Even if he gets off," Fish said. "That don't make him innocent."

"So you believe he's guilty because he comes from a crime family," she said. "Or because Jill Rykoff's prosecuting the case?"

There was a chorus of "Whoa!"

"What's wrong with you, Cooper? When did you get so sensitive?" Fish said.

She looked around the table. Ham's boyish face and graying beard, Sarge's mustache waxed to little points, Jerry's crinkly blues trained on her. Fish and now 2-K: these men were her family, the family she'd made. Everyone willing to believe Jill Rykoff based on the flimsiest of evidence. Everyone questioning her judgment.

"Cash me out," she told Ham.

CHAPTER 22

Early Tuesday morning Lennox stood at her office window watching the foot traffic across the street. Tomek had recognized the name Terry Purcell, but he was no good with phone numbers. Was Pieter making deliveries while Tomek was in jail? Was he selling to Terry Purcell?

Jeff Ito rang the bell outside. Asked Lennox to buzz him in.

Why?

"I have a favor to ask," he said. "Come on." He used that wheedling tone of voice some women must've found irresistible. Ito had very few moves, all enhanced by his gorgeousness, all of which he most likely developed before he hit grade school. The psychic was right when she told Cathy to get rid of this guy.

"Two minutes," she said. "I've got work to do."

He sat in her visitor chair looking bright and shiny, like a man who'd gone to bed sober the night before.

"You said a favor," she said.

Her phone rang.

Fish.

Fish never called during the day unless he had something for her. "I've got to take this," she said to Jeff.

"Jagoda's been shot," Fish said.

Her pulse raced. It took enormous effort to take in air. "Which Jagoda?" she said.

"Your client."

"How could that happen? He was in jail," she said.

Fish told her there was a computer error. Eleven prisoners early released. Tomek was one of them. Tomek went home. He was there maybe fifteen minutes when his next-door neighbor heard a loud pop and her dog went crazy. She went to investigate and found Tomek in his back yard.

"Is he dead?" Lennox held her breath. Waited for the confirmation that would break her heart.

"Not yet," Fish said. "He's in ICU. Providence Hospital, Glisan."

She grabbed her jacket. "Get out," she told Ito.

He looked at her with a blank expression. She pushed him out the door. Ran down the street to where her Bronco was parked. She called Kline on the way to the hospital and left him a voicemail about Tomek.

Tomek. A computer error? In all the years Lennox had worked in criminal justice she'd only heard of this kind of thing happening in the State of Washington, in a state prison. Who let him out? Who was lying in wait for him?

Tomek was in the ICU, fourth floor. Lennox hadn't set foot in a hospital since she and Fulin had been life-flighted to Emanuel. The headache that had started while she was driving to the hospital grew to adulthood by the time the glass doors parted and she entered the muted lobby. A volunteer at the information desk asked if Lennox was a relative. "Sister," Lennox told her. She took the elevator and walked down the highly waxed, blindingly bright hallway to the nurses' station. Lied to Nurse Debbie about being a relative as well. Lennox pointed to the glass-fronted room where a uniformed deputy sat by the door. A cop she didn't recognize. "That's Tomek's room?" Lennox said.

"He's in surgery," Debbie said. "You can wait with your family. The waiting room is down the hall and to your right."

"How is he?" Lennox asked.

"I haven't heard," Debbie said. Strictly professional. "The surgeon will come and talk to you when she's finished." If Lennox wasn't a fake Jagoda, if there wasn't a cop guarding Tomek's room, would the nurse have shown a little more sympathy?

She'd be waiting with the family. Lennox took several deep breaths, and shifted her pepper spray from her back jeans pocket to her jacket pocket, in case Pieter wanted to go mano a mano.

She found Idzi sitting against the wall next to a very old man. He looked asleep. Idzi looked like hell: red eyes, red nose, and still wearing a coat, though the room was over-heated. Three other families sat reading from their phones or talking with each other in low voices. Pieter was missing.

"I'm so sorry about Tomek," Lennox said. "I came right away. Idzi, you have to know I believe in Tomek. I care about him."

"He told me." Idzi blew her nose. "He told me how you cautioned him not to take the plea."

Tomek had talked to Kline, must've been yesterday, and turned down the plea. Then he was released and shot.

"What happened?" Lennox said.

"The jail called this morning. Said he'd been released on bail," Idzi said. "I went to the jail, paid the eleven-hundred dollars. I have the receipt." She pulled the paper from her handbag and showed it to Lennox. The receipt had been signed by Lennox's buddy, Doris. "He wanted to go home." Idzi's voice grew higher. "He worried about his bird feeders."

"They're saying something weird with the computers," Lennox said. "Ten other inmates were released in error."

"The other people that got out on bail, did they get shot?" Idzi said.

Bet your ass, nobody else. Who could get into the system but an insider? Who set up the bail? The whole deal was different from the computer glitch in Washington.

Dick the dick's case against Tomek was weak, which was the only reason the prosecutor offered a plea. Tomek refused the plea, and one day later he was let out of jail and shot. The killer was directing someone who worked at the jail. That, or the killer was the same person who engineered the early release.

"Who besides the cops at the jail knew Tomek had gone out on bail?" Lennox said.

"Just Pieter," Idzi said.

Just the jealous, violent brother. "Where is he?"

Pieter's wife was trying to find someone to take over at the bakery for her. Meanwhile Pieter was home with the kids.

A doctor walked in wearing what looked like a fresh pair of scrubs. She looked around the waiting room for the right family. Her hair was pulled back in a pony tail. Her young face was grave. "Mrs. Jagoda?" she said to the room. Idzi raised her hand and elbowed her husband, who blinked open his eyes. The doctor pulled an ottoman over to face them. "Mr. Jagoda?"

They shook hands. Her name was Dr. Weston. She looked at Lennox. Lennox introduced herself as Tomek's sister. She felt Idzi doing a double take, but like good crime mothers everywhere, she kept mum. The old man didn't seem to notice.

"Your son made it through surgery," Dr. Weston said.

Idzi and Lennox exhaled with relief. Mr. Jagoda nodded and smiled.

The surgeon explained that Tomek had been shot in the abdomen. "The biggest problem was damage to the vena cava. We'll have to hope the stitches hold. There are two holes and the tissue is shredded. And we repaired the intestine. That's all we could do for now," she said. "We'll need to go back in and resection the bowel."

"Is he going to make it?" Idzi sounded out of breath.

"He could," the doctor said. Out of that smooth face stared old kind eyes. "There's the chance of more bleeding and infection, but his heart is strong."

"Did you find the bullet?" Lennox asked.

Both Idzi and the surgeon turned to her.

The doctor exhaled. "Yeah. It's lodged in his spine." She glanced at Idzi. "It missed his spinal cord. We're thinking we'll leave it there, at least for now."

"Any guess what caliber bullet?" Lennox said.

Now the doctor looked truly puzzled. "My guess is a .22," the doctor said.

A .22 is a common-as-dirt starter rifle. Not a weapon an assassin would use.

"They'll be wheeling him back to ICU shortly. It'll be

around an hour before you can see him. Make sure you wear a mask."

She smiled and shook hands with Idzi. Mr. Jagoda had fallen asleep. The doctor shook hands with Lennox, studying her face, trying to get a bead on her.

Tomek had been mysteriously released and shot within an hour of being home. That was no coincidence. Tomek was in danger, and not just from his injuries. That cop watching him could be waiting for just the right moment to inject air into his vein. And what about Pieter? Pieter, who hadn't made an appearance yet.

"How far do you trust Pieter?" Lennox kept her voice low.

"He's my rock," Idzi said.

"He resents Tomek. He's jealous," Lennox said.

"We're family," Idzi said. "Where we come from, that's everything."

Lennox was going to have to take her word for it. Idzi, alone, was not enough to keep Tomek safe.

"Some cop, some person inside the system released those inmates," Lennox said. "How else did this happen?"

Idzi reached into that freaking crocodile handbag and pulled out a fresh handkerchief. Blew her nose.

"You're going to need to stay with Tomek," Lennox said. "Night and day."

"Pieter can help me," she said. "His wife. And we have good friends, family friends." Idzi's phone rang. Idzi spoke to the caller in Polish. "That was Pieter," she said. "They're on their way."

"Until the attorneys decide to postpone the trial, I have to keep working the case," Lennox said. She promised to call in. Promised she'd get to the bottom of Hadley's murder.

The minute the hospital doors closed behind her,

Lennox texted Shawn. No reply. So she called him. It immediately went to message. She called again. Okay, so she was obnoxious, but she wanted to know if the sheriff's department had solicited help from the Bureau. A text came back: "Stop. Busy." What did she expect from a guy she kept blowing off?

Fish didn't know a whole lot more beyond what he had told her already. "Is Jagoda dead yet?" he said. Even if Pope Francis made Tomek a saint, Fish was going to believe he was a murdering lowlife. Her next call went out to Sarge and hit his voicemail as well.

Sarge called her back just as Lennox reached her driveway. They agreed to meet at the Shanty in a half hour.

• • •

It was a lonely November evening at the Shanty. Only a handful of people sat at the bar watching a Nova program about deep sea creatures. The light was dim, the Halloween decorations gone. It smelled more like cleaning products than fried food. There wasn't a cop to be seen.

Lennox ordered a beer and a cup of chowder and chose a table far away from the bar and out of earshot. The bartender delivered her chowder just as Sarge walked in. His parka was unzipped halfway down, revealing a Harley Davidson tee shirt. His mustache looked newly waxed. He stopped at the bar to get a beer, then joined her at her table.

"The early release," he said.

Sarge, the cop whisperer. Nothing got past him. He'd been running the police evidence room since forever ago, and everybody trusted him. He even had ears in the Multnomah County Sheriff's Department.

"What have you heard?" she said.

Sarge took a long pull off his beer. "Eleven inmates total. Jagoda down. You knew that. How is he?" Sarge dabbed his mustache with his cocktail napkin.

"He's bad, Sarge. I don't know if he's going to make it. How did this happen?"

Sarge shook his shiny head. "They don't know. You remember the software problem up in Washington? That went on for thirteen years."

"Yeah, but Sarge, Tomek and the others were released on bail. That's an extra step."

"I know. All I can say is that the brass is investigating. Extra precautions."

"Tomek gets released and an hour later he's gunned down? C'mon."

"You're right, it's too much of a coincidence."

Lennox leaned closer and lowered her voice. "I'll tell you something else. You know that plea bargain the prosecutor offered Tomek? He turned it down yesterday. The next morning he was released and shot."

Sarge nodded unhappily. "It's not a glitch. Someone manipulated the computer."

"An insider," she said.

"But it's the sheriff's department that runs the jail. Sloane and Murdock work for the Portland Police."

"So what's your explanation?"

Sarge shook his head. She didn't have to say it. Sloane had worked with Tommy. Tommy was dirty, ergo—

"Let me think about it." He stood up, squeezed her shoulder. "Got to go," he said. "Don't want to worry my better half."

CHAPTER 23

Forget about the president and Congress, the headlines were all about the so-called computer error that allowed eleven inmates to walk free, three of them dangerous. A manhunt was in progress.

The glass walls in Kline's office suite looked out at the cloud squatting like a fat gray toad over the city. The air in the office was chilly as always. Emily, Kline's receptionist, the nice one, handed Lennox her coffee in a china cup.

"Watch out," Emily said under her breath. "He's in a bad mood."

Lennox could just imagine how Kline's meeting had gone when he'd presented the plea bargain to Tomek. And Kline would know that Tomek had been coached by her. She'd crossed the line by a block, and she didn't give a damn. Tomek had been fingered for Hadley's murder because he was a Jagoda, and once he refused his plea, he'd been shot. She wrapped her fingers around the coffee cup for warmth.

Emily pushed a button on her console. "Yes, Mr. Kline," she said. She nodded at Lennox. *Good luck*, she mouthed.

Lennox walked the eleven steps from Kline's office door to his gigantic desk. His face was tight and pissed off. The gold seals on his various degrees and certifications glittered behind their frames in the low light. He motioned her to sit.

"What you and I talk about in our meetings is confidential," he said. "I thought we were a team. Why the hell did you tip my hand?"

He'd been playing his hand; she'd been playing hers. He was the lawyer; he figured his hand ought to trump hers. But her hand was the right hand.

"Why are we talking confidentiality after what happened at the jail?" she said.

"Computer error." He was red-faced. "Now what? Jagoda's been shot. Our case is in the shitter. You deliberately sabotaged my meeting with Jagoda. If I don't agree with you, you just go ahead and do whatever the hell you want. You've been so much more trouble than anyone I've ever worked with."

Before Lennox, Kline had worked with various by-the-book detective agencies. If any one of them had a novel thought, they'd take it out and shoot it.

"If Calderbank is so great, so much less trouble, why do you keep working with me?"

Kline raked his hands through his curls and said nothing. It's scary when a lawyer goes silent on you.

"Are you going to pretend that everything that happened after Jagoda turned down your plea is a coincidence?" she said to get him arguing again, to get him to stop thinking about the good old days with Calderbank.

"Coincidences do happen. He's a drug dealer. In that world, people are getting shot all the time." Kline's voice was quiet now. She liked it better when he was shouting at her.

"If you had doubts about him before, everything in the last twenty-four hours should've convinced you he's innocent."

"You don't even understand what I'm doing here. I'm tasked with providing the best defense I can give."

"Assault three isn't the best defense. It's dog shit. Do you really think that it was an error that got Tomek an early release?" she said.

"I don't know. Unlike you, I don't have my gut instinct that tells me truth from fiction."

"Hadley made five calls the night of her murder. Two to Tomek, one to Slocum, one to a burner phone, one to Ito." She was talking faster and faster, wanting to explain herself, wanting him to understand. "The prosecution hit the wall when the burner was traced back to a Terry Purcell. Terry Purcell doesn't exist. But get this, Tomek has a customer named Terry Purcell. Don't you see? We're close."

"So what is it? A druggie or a cop that shot Jagoda?"

Lennox hadn't gotten that far. But she was close. She was very close. "You wouldn't have considered the plea bargain if it wasn't Jill Rykoff making the offer."

Why did she say it? Why did she even allow herself to think it? Only an idiot would double down when they were already in the deepest of shit.

He threw his hands up in the air. "Forget about Rykoff. You've had a bee in your bonnet about her from the beginning." He shook his head. "I don't know, Cooper. You've got talent, I know that. But there's something about you that invites trouble. You don't follow the rules, and on top of that, you've got a weird jealousy going when it comes to Jill. We've got two weeks until trial unless Jagoda dies. But if he does make it, he has you to blame if he's convicted."

Lennox couldn't bear to look at him anymore. It hurt too much. It wasn't just the job that was the world to her. It was him.

She stood up.

"I don't know if we can keep working together after this trial," Kline said.

Lennox couldn't believe he'd say something so cold. She left his office numb, as though all the chilly air in Kline's office and the fog on her way back to her truck had sunk deep into her bones. She'd never be warm again. Instead of driving back to the office, Lennox drove home, let Gretchen out, and fed her. She called Idzi. Tomek had taken a bad turn.

"Who's watching over him tonight?" Lennox said.

"Me."

"I can spell you," Lennox said. Idzi sounded too exhausted to put up much of an argument. Crazy. With everything that had happened, they'd become something that looked like friends.

CHAPTER 24

Morning light came through the hospital window. Another cold, gray day. Lennox threw off the thin blankets and stood up to stretch. Her left knee and hip were stiff and painful. All night, she had chewed over Kline: what he said, what she said. How many times in her life had her sense of rightness landed her in the shit.

At three o'clock in the morning, Tomek had had an "event." That's what they call it when your body hits bottom. His blood pressure had plummeted and set off a bunch of alarms. The staff rushed in and shooed Lennox out. The cop sitting next to Tomek's door looked straight ahead, showing no interest in what was going on in Tomek's room. Lennox asked him his name, and he shot her a filthy look, probably thinking she was Tomek's sister and therefore criminal scum.

The doctor was able to give Tomek something that stabilized him, and the alarms quieted. Eventually, the doctor left. Ten minutes later, the nurses left as well.

"Nice meeting you," Lennox said to the deputy.

But this morning, Tomek was sleeping peacefully. The respirator whirred, a series of two beats and a Darth Vader hiss. Tomek didn't stir. Not even his eyelids twitched with dreams. Pale skin, pale hair, he was colorless except for the ink on his right arm: a spiraling tree branch, green leaves, orange and blue birds. Tomek took up every square inch of the hospital bed and more, his feet hanging over the side.

The nurse walked in. Replaced the names of the duty nurse, CNA and the doctor on the whiteboard. Told Lennox to step out so she could attend to her patient. Lennox hurriedly helped herself to some nasty looking coffee at the nurses' station before standing outside the door opposite the asshole cop. Five minutes later, the nurse was finished.

Lennox sipped the coffee, executed a series of neck rolls, and looked up to see Pieter standing in the doorway in a leather biker jacket, blond hair standing in just-showered spikes. He looked as exhausted as she felt.

"Get," he said.

"Don't you want to know how he's doing?"

"He's on a respirator in the ICU," Pieter said. "That's how he's doing."

She and Pieter had to get beyond their mutual hatred and distrust for one another and start working together. She was taking her chances walking up to a violent man chin to chin, a guy who had no qualms about hitting a woman. Standing close enough to smell his cigarette breath, his drugstore aftershave, she pointed at the police guard stationed on the other side of the wall.

"I need to talk to you," she said in a low voice.

He made a disgusted face and shook his head.

"How do you know the shooter won't go after you

next?" she whispered. She went to the corner of the room furthest from the door.

He remained where he stood, glaring at her from the doorway.

She folded her arms across her chest. She'd been up all night, but she'd stand there all morning unless Pieter answered her questions.

Finally, he came over to her.

"Who do you think did this?" She pointed to Tomek.

He snorted.

"Who?"

"The cops, who do you think?" he said in a hoarse whisper, his acrid breath in Lennox's face. "Have you been over to his house? There's no crime scene tape. No nothing. Those fuckers aren't even investigating this."

What the hell? "Maybe the forensics people have come and gone."

He gave her that don't-even-try look. Tomek's respirator beeped and hissed. "The cops in this town would love for all our family to end up dead."

"A cop wouldn't use a .22 to take Tomek out. I figure it's got to be one of your customers. One that had a cop in his pocket. Hadley called a Terry Purcell twice the night of her murder. You know him?"

"You think you can come in here acting all concerned and I'm going to tell you things? I'm not the one that's stupid."

"But Hadley," she said. "Somehow Tomek's shooter is connected to Hadley."

"You cops," he said. "Always with the patterns. Shit happens. End of story."

"Think about it," she said.

"Yeah, sure."

Lennox picked up a coffee and a scone at the kiosk in the hospital lobby. Had a long and satisfying pee in the lobby restroom before leaving the hospital and driving to Tomek's house. The local news on her truck radio buzzed with the tale of ten fugitives at large from Portland's jail. The PR woman for the sheriff's department was calling it a computer glitch and promising a full investigation once the inmates were found and secured. She hinted that the fault was due to Tony White, the city council's budget expert not giving them the "necessary resources to run their department." Lennox wondered how many heads would roll.

She got to Tomek's house. The blinds were open, his door was locked. She walked down the gravel walk that led to his back yard. An empty bird feeder lay on its side on the grass, the patch beneath it stained with what Lennox was sure was Tomek's blood. What had Kline said? Something about the world of drug dealers. How could anyone who really knew Tomek think he had this coming?

Pieter was right about the crime scene. No tape. No evidence of a police investigation. The cops would love to see the Jagodas dead.

• • •

Lennox canvassed the neighbors closest to Tomek's house. Sylvia Blench, Tomek's next-door neighbor, was the one who'd found him. She was somewhere in her seventies. Wore old lady clothes, not boutique like the kind of stuff Idzi wore, but old lady pants, a flowered top and a twenty-dollar haircut. Sylvia thought maybe she had heard a crack.

But it had been her dog, Robert, who would not quit barking until she investigated. She went on and on about Robert and what a smart dog he was, and about Tomek, how he'd mowed her grass and raked her leaves, wouldn't take her money. She talked about the bird sanctuary in his back yard. Sylvia made him sound like a Polish St. Francis. He *was* St. Francis—if St. Francis dealt dope for his mother. "Don't tell me he's dead," Sylvia said. "I couldn't stand it." She didn't believe all the terrible things they said about Tomek when they arrested him for his girlfriend's murder.

Had the police talked to her about the shooting? Yes, but the policeman wasn't a dog person. In fact, he made Sylvia put Robert in the back room, even though it was Robert who saved Tomek's life. Sylvia had so much more to say. Getting off her doorstep was like trying to come unstuck from a big wad of chewing gum.

The rest of the neighbors within earshot of a .22 were as old or older than Ms. Sylvia. No one had heard the shot. That was the thing about .22s. They didn't make a whole lot of noise. None of the neighbors had noticed any strangers. When she'd exhausted the neighborhood, Lennox called Sarge. He told her that Detective Derek Murdock had been tasked with investigating Tomek's shooting.

"What kind of a cop is he?" she said. "There's no crime scene tape. No sign anyone's been here."

"It's stretched pretty thin here," Sarge said in a tight voice.

Maybe Pieter was right, shooting a Jagoda was low on the list of police priorities. Lennox asked for Murdock's telephone number.

"I don't have time for this," Sarge said in a testy voice. "There's a manhunt going on."

"You can give me Murdock's number or stay on the phone arguing with me," she said.

Sarge gave her the number on condition that she didn't reveal who gave it to her.

The call to Murdock went immediately to voicemail. So she drove downtown to Central Precinct. Five reporters from the local stations, and their attendant cameramen and support dudes and dudettes clogged the granite steps. Lennox bobbed and ducked her way up the stairs.

She was asked her name and business three times after she passed through security. The second-floor bullpen was nearly empty of cops. Lennox spotted Shawn in a heated exchange with another officer. He didn't notice her.

The officer at the duty desk pointed to Derek Murdock hunched over a laptop, four-finger typing. The hem of his sports coat brushed the floor from the chair back. She pegged him to be in his early forties and thirty pounds overweight, and that was being kind.

Lennox introduced herself. Told him that she was the detective working on the Jagoda defense.

"Uh huh," he said. His mouth seemed too small for his face.

"I just got back from Tomek's house. It doesn't look like you've been out there," she said.

"Are you trying to tell me how to run an investigation?"

Lennox could tell from his tone that she had about thirty seconds before he escorted her out of the room. "You're aware of how weird it looks that Tomek was let out of jail, then shot less than an hour later, and that there's no sign of an investigation going on."

Murdock blinked at her impertinence. "Trust me, lady. We're looking into it," he said.

"Can you tell me what you've found so far?"

"You got to be kidding me," he said.

Shawn and the officer he was arguing with strode out the door. If he saw Lennox, he made no show of it. "Any word yet how my client was released from jail?" she said to Murdock.

"I'm sure you've heard that the matter is being investigated." He stood up, all six feet of him and stepped very close to her. She looked up at the folds of flesh where his chin should be. "We're very busy just now, so if you could see yourself out."

She took a step back so she could see him. He had unreadable cop eyes.

"You've managed to keep the Jagoda shooting out of the news so far. But there's a mob of reporters and cameramen camped on your doorstep."

His body tensed like he was ready to launch himself at her. "Are you threatening me?"

"I'll go first," she said. "Tomek has a bullet lodged in his spine. His surgeon's pretty sure he was hit by a .22."

He pulled a notebook from his desk drawer and wrote something, then slowly leaned back in his chair. "No bullet casings were found. The gravel on the side of the house was trampled by the first responders."

He shook his head. "No fingerprints other than Jagoda's. The house was locked and looked undisturbed. The garage door was open. It's not a lot to go on. And we don't have much in the way of resources at present."

And what resources they had were not going to be spent on finding Tomek's shooter. Pieter was right. She'd seen the Bureau make more effort trying to track a stolen car.

CHAPTER 25

Random events come out of nowhere and blindside a person, and there are times when a body can't make sense of it. But Lennox couldn't believe that the connection between Tomek's shooting and Hadley's death was just random coincidence. What the two events had in common was drugs. But how did that tie in with someone in law enforcement engineering Tomek's release? She needed someone she trusted to bounce ideas off. Someone who worked with patterns, someone like a forensic accountant. Ham agreed to meet her at her house at ten the following morning.

Lennox was still in pajamas when Ham showed up at her door. He held a Starbucks in each hand, his briefcase tucked under his arm.

Gretchen announced his arrival with a chorus of barking. "Quiet," Lennox said. A blast of cold air hit her as she opened the door. Dead leaves chased stray trash along the sidewalk outside her house.

"Late night?" Ham said, setting the Starbucks and his briefcase on the dining room table.

"Yeah," she said. "This case is kicking my butt."

He sat down. Gretchen sat beside him. He scratched behind Gretchen's ears. She licked his fingers and grinned that doggy grin of hers. "Where's your cookies?" He used the same sing-song voice Kline took with the dog. Now that he was ready to write Lennox off, she wondered if Kline would take Gretchen back.

"What's up with you?" Ham said. "You look like you're going to cry."

She shook her head. The dog bounded into the kitchen.

"I'll be right back," Ham said.

He was gone just long enough for Lennox to pull herself together. She told him everything she had so far.

"You don't think this is a case of shit happens, do you?" she said.

He shook his head. "Too many coincidences."

Lennox relaxed further into her chair. She hadn't realized how Kline, Pieter, and every cop she'd talked to were wearing her down with their skepticism.

"I've pretty much ruled Ito out," she said. "I can totally see him drowning Hadley, but he's too dumb to have orchestrated the prisoner release."

"You saw Slocum talking to the chief of police the night of Kline's charity thingy?" Ham said.

"Yeah, and I did more research into his finances and found he's quite a philanthropist when it comes to police charities."

"He writes scripts for painkillers and amphetamines," Ham said. "He's the victim's doctor. She called him the night of her murder. And it's easy to believe that he'd have some cop in his pocket. What's his motive?"

"I'm thinking blackmail."

"What about his alibi?" Ham said.

"He and his wife were at Timberline Lodge for the weekend. Of course, he could've gotten the call from Hadley, driven back to town, and then back up the mountain before morning."

Ham looked over the top of his reading glasses. "Tells his wife, sorry honey, I got to murder somebody, I'll be back for breakfast? Did you check it out?" Ham said.

"Not yet."

"You've ruled out Ito and his girlfriend. You've ruled out the Jagodas," Ham said. "You've got Slocum and the Terry guy?"

"Terry Purcell. The fake name on a burner phone. Tomek recognized his name as a customer. I figured Pieter might recognize the name, too. But he won't give me a thing, even with his brother fighting for his life. He thinks I'm going to have him busted for dealing."

"What can I do to help?" Ham said.

"Just bouncing ideas off you is great," she said. "It's obvious the prosecution fluffed the rundown on Terry Purcell and tracking the burner phone."

"Do you know how many stores sell cheap phones, or how many transactions are cash?"

"But you have to activate the phone from a phone," she said. "And that number is always attached to the burner."

"I hope you're not suggesting we try to run down the phone. We'd have to go through how many carriers for how many phones?" Ham took his glasses off and rubbed his eyes. "Don't forget you're in the private sector now. No phone carrier's going to turn their records over to you."

"Verizon and AT&T are the main carriers. We could start with those. There's got to be a way."

She was wrung out and desperate. Not enough sleep, not enough answers. "I'm running out of time," she said. "I'll run surveillance on Pieter in the hopes that one of his customers is Terry Purcell. If I could tie a license plate number to the phone number, then we've got Terry as a solid contender. And I'll check out the Slocum alibi."

Ham folded his glasses, gathered up his notebooks and pencils, and tucked them in his briefcase. "I guess that leaves me with the burner detail." He pulled himself out of the chair, weary already at the thought of running down the number.

"Your hours will go on my expense report," she said.

"You better believe it," he said. He pulled his jacket on. Rubbed his knuckles across her scalp. They'd be old people moving around with walkers, and he'd still treat her like his kid sister.

"Thanks Ham."

He lifted his hand in salute and left.

She bolted the door behind him. Considered breakfast before a shower. The low November sun reached across the living room and halfway up the wall. The room smelled faintly of ash where the wind had found its way down her chimney. Her mail arrived on the porch. A phone bill, a flyer, and an oversized envelope from the medical board.

The Slocum report.

She opened the envelope to see page after page of blacked out lines, like Slocum was a spy. What was she supposed to do with this?

Lennox punched the number of her friend, the coroner.

"It's Cooper," Samantha said. "The girlfriend who only calls when she needs something."

"I swear when I get done with this case, I'll buy you dinner."

Lennox heard a grunt on the other end of the line. "What do you want?"

"I requested a report from the medical board on a murder suspect who ran afoul of the board three years ago."

Sam interrupted her, "The murder of the little lady floating in a hot tub?"

"That's the one," Lennox said. "Anyway, the report looks like a CIA document. The whole thing is blacked out."

"It means the doc is currently under investigation," Sam said.

Lennox thanked her and made many promises for food and drink. Slocum was still under investigation. If Hadley had threatened to claim that he got her addicted to painkillers then traded sex for pills, his practice, his marriage, and possibly his freedom would be in the toilet.

• • •

Lennox rented a silver Toyota Camry. Short of painting herself in invisible paint, the Camry made her unidentifiable. Late afternoon, she drove to Pieter's address and parked four car lengths down the street from his house. It was still sunny. Piles of brown leaves lay heaped along the curb. Crows picked along the edges of the raked leaves looking for worms. Pieter's truck was parked in the driveway, the blinds open in his front window.

Lennox ate a couple of energy bars and watched his children come home from school in their parochial school uniforms. An hour later Pieter's wife pulled into their driveway, her pink waitress smock beneath her unbuttoned coat. The sun had set.

At 7:30, Pieter left the house in his wife's Mercedes and drove west across the bridge. Lennox followed him, staying as far back as she dared. Better to lose him and follow him tomorrow than to get caught. He drove south and took the Terwilliger exit. Through steep hillsides, trees hugging the narrow road, she climbed the dark streets up to the West Hills. Pieter turned left onto a narrow road and then right where a street sign announced a dead end. Lennox hung back and waited after Pieter's headlights turned off. She parked her car facing down the hill and followed on foot along the narrow road where Pieter had driven. The road climbed a steep hill and ended in a circular driveway. A large stone house clung to the wooded hillside. The Slocums'.

Lennox crouched behind the shrubbery, back from the driveway. The door opened and a thick-set man left the house, climbed into a black SUV, and backed out of the driveway. Ten minutes later the door opened again and Pieter left. He climbed back into the Mercedes and drove off. Lennox ran back to her car and caught up with him as he drove down Terwilliger Road.

From there he crossed the Hawthorne Bridge south to Powell and headed east. She tailed him past blocks of strip malls until the neighborhoods thinned, then along a flat swath of land dotted with strip bars and wrecking yards. The fir trees that anchored the landscape heaved in the wind. Lennox spotted a sign set high above the power lines: *Lumpy's Bar* in blinding white and red script. Pieter parked in the back corner of the parking lot. Ten minutes later, a 1980s Chevy Caprice pulled in next to the Mercedes. Not so much a car as a boat. She wrote down the license plate number. The driver waddled over to Pieter's car, knocked against the car. Pieter powered down the window and an exchange was made that looked as if they were clumsily shaking hands. The Caprice drove away.

Lennox recorded fourteen exchanges over the next three hours and wrote down all their license plate numbers. At midnight, Pieter left and drove to the hospital.

Lennox headed home.

CHAPTER 26

Tomek's shooting was everywhere on the news that morning. *Tomek Jagoda was one of the inmates freed in the mysterious early release at Multnomah County Jail. Charged with murder, Jagoda was never a candidate for bail. Two other inmates charged with violent crimes are still at large.* Blah-blah, *the sheriff's department is investigating...*

Murdock was going to think she leaked Tomek's shooting. Her head throbbed. Lennox swallowed two aspirin with her Americano, extra shot of espresso, and opened her computer. She had fourteen license plate numbers to check out, data diving hoping to tie one of these people with the Terry Purcell alias. Rain pelted against her office windows. Someone was burning essential oils down the hall.

Her intercom hissed. It was Jeff Ito. Now that Lennox had written him off as a suspect, she had no use for him.

"What do you want?" she said.

He told her he was in terrible trouble. Some crap about Cathy, no doubt. "You've got three minutes," she said and buzzed him in. He had a cut on his lip and a butterfly bandage across one cheek. His clothes looked like he'd slept in them. Booze sweated out his pores and stunk up the place.

"I'm glad rehab is working for you," she said.

He flopped into her visitor chair without being asked to sit down. That was Jeff all over again.

"Don't get too comfortable," she said.

"I don't know what to do," he said. "Cathy's going to get me arrested."

"Why are you even here?" she said. She could hardly bear to look at him, much less smell him. He was hopeless.

"So I went to Cathy's to pick up my things. She knew I was coming, we'd settled on a time. I show up, she flies at me like out of *Fatal Attraction*. All nails and teeth. You see what she's done to my face. And she bit me." He rolled up the sleeve on his hoody to show bite marks on his forearm.

"And then what?" Lennox said with all the weariness that came from lack of sleep and a ton of stress.

"I tried to fend her off. She was hurting me," he said.

"You hit her," Lennox said, knowing the worst-case scenario was the probable scenario.

"I had to defend myself," he said. "She fell against her coffee table. Cut herself right on the cheekbone. I didn't hit her."

"Did she call the cops?"

His eyes widened. "They called me last night. Told me to come in. Asked me if I had threatened to kill her. That's what she told them. That I threatened to kill her."

"Did you?"

"Of course not," he said. "Maybe I said some things."

"Maybe you'd been drinking," she said.

He shook his head.

"C'mon," she said. "I can smell it on you."

"Am I going to jail?" he said in a shaky little voice.

"It's possible," she said. "Do you have an attorney?"

"My lawyer does only real estate. I tried calling you, but you didn't answer your phone."

Said as if it was her fault he was in trouble. Somehow in his alcohol-addled brain he thought she was his little helper bee. The guy was an idiot. Could he have gotten himself in a rage, slipped on gloves and held Hadley's head under water? Absolutely. But Lennox still couldn't imagine him tracking down Tomek. Even less likely was the notion that Jeff had a cop in his pocket.

"I thought maybe you could give me a referral?" he continued.

"I know some good criminal attorneys," she said.

Jeff pulled out his phone and looked at her expectantly.

"Tell me who you buy drugs from," she said.

"I'm clean," Jeff said. Sweat shone near his temples.

"Yeah. Clean and sober." She stood up and walked to the door. "Go home, Jeff."

"You've got to help me," he said.

She stood at the door with her hand on the doorknob. "You want me to help you, you have to help me."

He jumped to his feet. "I'm not doing coke anymore. That's the fucking truth," he said. He ran his hand through his hair. Then he gave his head a little shake so the hair fell in a perfect tousle.

She took a deep breath and waited for him to stop posing.

"You don't know what it's been like for me," he said.

"Time's up," she said, keeping her hand on the doorknob. With luck it might yield something she could use.

But still he blathered about the shock of finding Hadley's body. He thought maybe he had PTSD.

"You got to be kidding me," she said.

"Abby Slocum never liked me," he said. "Once the psychic started saying bad things, Abby jumped in with her two cents. Not only is our engagement off, now Cathy is trying to get me arrested."

Lennox motioned him out the door.

"I got a script for Oxys." His voice wheedling and desperate.

"From?"

"Slocum."

Finally, finally the guy came up with something useful. Why had it taken him this long? "You said you didn't know Dr. Slocum," she said.

"I don't know him *per se*. He used to date Hadley years ago."

"Say that again," Lennox said.

"They went out for three, four years. He was the one who got her started using. Then he dumped her for the trophy bitch."

But she still was getting prescriptions from him. Lennox asked if it was possible that Hadley was blackmailing Slocum.

Jeff seemed certain that Slocum and Hadley had remained friends. This was huge.

"So maybe Abby was jealous of Hadley, as well?"

Jeff's eyes lit up and he nodded. Another person to take the blame.

Lennox asked him what he knew about Abby. He gave her a few details about how Abby spent her time, but he seemed to sag under all the truth-telling. She gave him some phone numbers of decent defense attorneys.

"What about the guy you're working for?" he said.

"That would be a conflict," she said. "You're still high on our suspect list."

It was very satisfying to watch her words sink in.

She closed the door behind him.

• • •

If Slocum had a dirty cop in his pocket, could that extend to Abby as well? Jeff had said that Abby divided her day between the gym and the yoga studio. He also said that Abby knew that her husband used to date Hadley. So could it be that Hadley was blackmailing Abby's husband? Or sleeping with him?

DMV records, a look-see on social media and a couple of phone calls later, Lennox decided to try her luck finding Abby Slocum at the Blossoming Lotus yoga studio in John's Landing. She found Abby's Jaguar amongst a herd of Subarus. Abby's Jag was a new model XFS in British Racing Green, the only color for a Jag, in Lennox's opinion. The studio was a two-story cedar-sided building with tall windows on the second story. While she waited for Abby to finish her class, she shuffled the tarot cards and cut them. A reversed Knight of Cups. She turned the card right side up and studied it. He looked a lot like a one-eyed jack arriving on a white horse, offering a glass of wine. But reversed, the card meant deception, emotional immaturity, an escapist personality. Jeff Ito, at the heart of everything. She knew the type. Every woman over thirty knew the type.

Several car fobs chirped at once as a group of skinny

women in Lycra fanned out from the studio door to their respective cars. Lennox hurriedly tucked the tarot deck back in its box and watched for Abby. She came out in the second wave of women. Lennox recognized her from all the pics on social media. She was blonde with delicate features, six-foot, and stick thin with big boobs. Ten to one the tits were add-ons.

Before Lennox could reach her, Abby had folded herself into the sports car and swung into traffic.

Lennox butted her way through the parking lot, ruining more than one woman's Zen attitude, jumped in her truck, and drove fast and recklessly until she caught sight of the Jag. She followed Abby all the way into the West Hills.

Back at the Slocum house again. Parked in the driveway were two SUVs, both black, both shiny, both huge, and Abby's Jag.

Abby, in her size two yoga tights, walked over to Lennox's truck, her face puzzled.

"May I help you?" she said.

Lennox flipped open her detective license. "I'm working on the Hadley Eberhart murder," she said. "Can we talk about Hadley and your husband?"

Abby's pupils constricted behind emerald green colored contacts. Another add-on. "Todd!" she yelled.

One second Abby and Lennox were chatting in the driveway, the next second two large characters appeared three yards in front of them. Lennox knew dubious when she saw it. These guys were felons, she'd put money on it. Todd and associate were most likely security.

They stood legs apart, hands at the ready. Were they armed?

Lennox waved both hands in a meant-no-harm gesture

and retreated to her truck. She rolled down her window and snapped photos of both guys. "Already sent," she shouted just as they started moving towards her truck. But Lennox was queen of the quick exit. She put the Bronco in gear and got the hell out of there.

So Abby didn't give her an interview. No Portland trophy wife that she knew of employed thugs for protection. This little scene spoke volumes about Abby's knowledge of her husband's associates. All it would take was too many calls from Hadley to her husband. Lennox could imagine Abby deploying her security over to Jeff's house. They drowned Hadley. The doc was buddies with the chief of police. It was easy to imagine that he had a cop in his pocket willing to set up early release on a bunch of inmates. Easy to jump from there to Tomek getting shot.

CHAPTER 21

Lennox forwarded the photos of Abby's security guys to Sarge with a message to call her. Then she gassed up the truck. It was four in the afternoon. The sun hadn't set, not technically, but she needed her headlights and her windshield wipers. Not the best time to head up the mountain, but Beth, the desk clerk at Timberline Lodge, was working tonight. And she had verified that she'd worked the night of October 9th.

The traffic lightened by the time Lennox reached Highway 26, eastbound. Sarge called back. What was he supposed to do with the photos Lennox had sent him?

"Run them through your database?"

Silence.

"Sarge?" she said. "Are you still there?" She got Sarge's lecture about police procedure, county time and resources. Blah-blah.

"These guys are security. They threatened me," she said. Which earned her two inches on the Pinocchio-meter. Abby's thugs had given her dirty looks and approached her vehicle like they might've wanted to harm her phone. The mini-lie produced the desired effect. Sarge turned all protective and solicitous. He told her he'd run the one photo through the database. The other photo was a guy he recognized: an ex-cop named Bill Jennings. She thanked Sarge and reassured him that she was living a risk-free life, not to worry.

The rain turned to snow by the time she reached Zigzag. The higher she climbed the harder it snowed. Occasionally she passed a slow-moving semi, but otherwise there was no traffic on the road and no snow plows. Lennox stopped at Government Camp and chained up. There were signs of life at the Ratskeller, but otherwise the village looked deserted. It was a black night and snowing hard. She emptied the last of her de-icer on the windshield and drove the twisty road up to Timberline.

Lennox pulled into Timberline's unplowed parking lot and walked the last treacherous bit from the lot to the front steps of the lodge. Twice she fell on her butt. Maybe cowboy boots were not the best choice for the mountain.

It was a relief to be inside, out of the snow, where there was wood and stone and nary a snowflake. A middle-aged couple held hands and watched the fire burning and snapping in the stone fireplace. The lodge was built by the WPA from the mountain's rock and timber. The WPA craftsmen and women carving and weaving and forging all the lodge's details had made Timberline Oregon's most beautiful building.

Beth Stanley stood behind the front desk. It was hard to judge Beth's age. She looked to be one of those people who spent most of the day's sunlight outdoors. She was tan and attractive, with a white-white smile that had never seen a cup of coffee. Lennox showed Beth her license and ID and told her that she worked for August Kline, gave her one of Kline's business cards. Handing off an attorney's business card along with her investigator's license lent her an air of officialdom. The business card wasn't quite as great as a badge, but as close as she was ever going to get again. And it worked. Beth studied Kline's card and seemed ready to waive any precautions about the guests' confidentiality.

Lennox asked Beth to check the registration for the night of October 9th.

Yes, Dr. James Slocum and his wife, Abby, had stayed the weekend in question. Beth identified both the doc and Abby from Lennox's photo arrays.

"So you remember them?"

Beth made an oops face and shrugged. "This is an old place. You can hear through the walls, and the couples on either side of the Slocums called down here to complain."

"They were fighting or having sex?" Lennox said.

"Fighting. I had to send maintenance up to their room to ask them to please keep it down."

Were they fighting over the call Hadley made to the doc that night?

"Then what happened?" Lennox said.

"Dr. Slocum slammed out."

Slammed out. It was like the skies opened and the voices of heavenly choirs sang OHM, or whatever heavenly choirs sang.

"Dr. Slocum left the lodge?"

Beth nodded solemnly. "I'd say around eleven? But I know when he got back because our door was locked."

"What time?"

"He called the desk to let him in at four o'clock in the morning."

Bingo.

Lennox thanked her and asked her if they had a room for the night.

• • •

The maintenance crew had plowed Timberline's parking lot by the time Lennox left the next morning. She had a blue-skied drive back on a plowed road to Portland. She stopped to feed Gretchen and make herself some breakfast. Even though Ham had fed Gretchen supper the night before, Gretchen gave Lennox a sorrowful brown-eyed stare when she left the house.

Lennox drove up into the West Hills, the fir trees by the side of the narrow road heaving in the wind, branches and needles scattering across the pavement. She arrived at the Slocum house and parked behind an SUV. Leaves rattled across the brick driveway.

Todd, the security thug, answered the door on the second ring. His mean little eyes flashed recognition. "What are you doing here?" he asked her.

She'd come to see Dr. Slocum. He asked if she had an appointment. She told him that the doc would want to see her. "Because?" he said.

"Just tell him."

Todd stood there like a big dumb oak and thought about it. Meanwhile, the cold bit her wrists and her cheeks. Her nose started running. She dug through her bag for a tissue. Todd eyed her suspiciously and reached behind his back, presumably for a gun she guessed was tucked in his waistband.

"Easy, cowboy," she said. She waved the tissue in front of him. "Tell him it's the connection between Hadley Eberhart and the medical board."

He nodded and shut the door in her face. It was unclear whether he was going to give Dr. Slocum her message. It was unclear whether the doc was even home. Meanwhile she was freezing her ass off. Kline's business card wouldn't cut any ice with Todd.

She shifted from foot to foot on the paved step, looked at her watch again. Five very long minutes staring at the door with no idea whether Todd would ever let her in. It was a nice wood door with a high window and a shiny brass handle. She kicked it with the heel of her boot. She kicked the door again and again. It got her circulation going.

Todd opened the door and asked her what the hell she was doing. "Am I seeing him or not?" she said.

"Don't make any trouble," he said. He led her through a white tiled foyer to a huge living room.

The doc was sitting on the edge of a hard-looking sofa upholstered in emerald green. The room was done up in mid-century furniture: lacquered tables shaped like kidney beans, green upholstered chairs on chrome legs, orange throw pillows, a painting on the wall behind the sofa that looked like a big block of green, a wall clock with long chrome rays. The wall facing the sofa had an unobstructed view of the north end of downtown Portland: towers and lofts, their glass windows blue-gray in the sunlight, traffic motoring across the Steel and Burnside Bridges.

The doctor motioned to an orange tweed chair facing

the sofa. It was as uncomfortable as it looked. "It would've been better if you'd made an appointment," he said.

Lennox reached in her bag and showed him her investigator license. He waved it away without glancing at it.

"I'm working on the Tomek Jagoda defense team."

"What does that have to do with me?" he said.

"You don't know the Jagodas?"

He looked at his watch and then back at her. "Just what I read in the paper."

"Pieter Jagoda made a stop here night before last."

He stiffened. "I don't know what you're talking about."

"I have a picture." She scrolled down her phone until she located it. "See?"

He waved the phone away without looking. "I don't have control over who drives up my driveway or rings my doorbell."

"Then why do you have a couple of bodyguards?"

He blinked his eyes as if he could barely endure answering her stupid fucking questions. "Anything else?" he said.

"Yes," she said. "You treated me. Don't you remember?"

He shook his head. He truly didn't look as if he recognized her.

"You wrote a script for painkillers and speed," she said.

He shook his head. "Doesn't ring a bell."

"You're being investigated by the medical board," she said.

His eyes turned cold. "That's confidential."

"I'm a detective."

He wasn't impressed. "I still don't know what that has to do with the Jagoda defense."

The front door swung open and a stream of frigid air

curled around their knees. Abby Slocum, dressed all in black, strode into the living room on high-heeled boots, carrying several bags from Mercantile and Mario's.

Her emerald green eyes glazed to furious points at the sight of Lennox sitting across from her husband. She dropped the bags at her feet.

"What is she doing here?"

The doc looked from Abby to Lennox. "You know each other?"

"Not really," Abby said.

"Why don't you put your new things away and let me handle this," the doc said to Abby. His smile couldn't soften the fact that he'd just told her to go upstairs and play, the men needed to talk.

"I have a few questions for Abby as well," Lennox said.

"Abby, go upstairs," the doc said, in a voice used to being obeyed.

"No," Abby said. She plopped herself on the sofa next to him and placed her hand on his knee, an enormous diamond glinting in the fading light. "Jim, I don't want you to talk to her, either. All she wants is someone to blame for that woman's death."

That woman's death. The doctor grimaced for a microsecond and then his features smoothed to self-possession. The reaction was so fleeting that Lennox almost didn't catch it. Did he care about Hadley Eberhart?

"The reason you were initially considered a 'person of interest' by the police in the Eberhart murder was a bottle of OxyContin with your name as the prescriber on the label," Lennox said.

"Todd," Abby shouted.

190

Like a genie from the lamp, Todd appeared from nowhere.

"Missus?" he said.

The doctor waved him off. He disappeared.

"Hadley called you at ten o'clock the night of October 9, while you and Abby were staying at Timberline Lodge," Lennox said to the doctor. "Did she want a prescription refill?"

Abby's hands balled in fists. "A patient, you said." Abby's hands clenched against her knees. "You sonuvabitch."

"You're overreacting," the doc told Abby. "It wasn't like that."

It didn't seem possible that Abby was unaware of Hadley's continued friendship with Slocum.

Lennox decided to test the theory. "Hadley and your husband stayed friends. She was over here a bunch of times, every time you went out of town." A total guess on Lennox's part.

"You sonuvabitch," Abby's voice tightened.

"You don't understand," Slocum told his wife.

Never tell a woman she doesn't understand, especially if she's white-hot pissed.

"What were you fighting about at Timberline Lodge if it wasn't about Hadley?" Lennox said.

"You told me she was history," Abby said.

Slocum grabbed his wife by the wrist. "Shut up," he said in a quiet voice. Just as quickly as he'd grabbed her, he released her wrist. Abby rubbed where he'd grabbed her, her eyes filling with tears. It seemed like all she cared about was whether her husband was schtupping Hadley. She wasn't the murderer. She wasn't the one who left Timberline Lodge in the middle of the night.

"Todd," the doc said. Todd appeared. The genie vanished, he reappeared…it was uncanny. Did he lurk around corners? Hide in the bushes?

"Remove her," Slocum told Todd.

Todd took Lennox by the arm and jerked her off the orange tweed chair.

"I'll get a subpoena," Lennox said.

"The hell you will," Slocum said. He flapped his hand and shooed her away.

Lennox started home. A quarter mile from the Slocums' house, a black and white passed her on the narrow road headed up the hill. She caught the shape of a head and could've sworn it was Shawn.

CHAPTER 28

Lennox drove back to Hadley's in Goose Hollow the following morning. She needed tangible proof: something, anything that proved that Hadley had been blackmailing Slocum. The sky darkened and it began raining again. The air had a bite to it.

Two men in stained sleeping bags lay on the tiled entrance of the Winston Apartments, crammed against the front door to shelter from the weather. Lennox wasn't crazy about the idea of stepping over them and picking the lock, but then a middle-aged woman in a belted raincoat pushed the door against them from the inside. A chorus of "sorry, sorry, sorry." The homeless guys struggled to emerge from their bags like dazed, smelly pupae.

The woman in the raincoat pushed out of the building and Lennox slid in. She climbed the flight of stairs and let herself into Hadley's apartment with her lock files. The room smelled stale from dead air and Hadley's dirty clothes hamper.

Lennox had been through every book, every cereal box,

the refrigerator, the freezer, her pantry, even under window sills. She'd checked every freaking place she knew to look, but somewhere in this apartment was the thing Hadley used to blackmail the doctor.

Lennox struggled with the old window and finally was able to raise it a foot. A gust of cold air hit her, drops of rain scattering along the sill. She looked around the studio for an opened seam in the mattress or a space beneath the bookcases. She went through every page of Hadley's three hundred and twelve page manuscript and the box it was stored in, every pocket of every piece of clothing. She examined the floor and baseboards for seams.

A toilet flushed upstairs, a tenor sang from *The Sound of Music* down the hall.

Hadley would've had to be clever hiding the blackmail she used against Slocum. Slocum was wily. His two thugs, especially Jennings, the ex-cop, were probably just as good as Lennox at finding hiding spots. She shoved her hand down the garbage disposal and felt around the blades for foreign objects. Pulled out all the knives in the knife block, shining her flashlight down the narrow cracks where they nested. She opened Hadley's silverware drawer and examined everything in the utensil drawer. She lined up each piece on the counter. Wine corks scattered amongst the rest of the spatulas and spoons. Hadley seemed to favor Chardonnays: Clos du Bois, Chateau Saint Michelle. One cork labeled Napa Valley Porchfest 2015 was virgin, no hole drilled through the top of it with a corkscrew. Lennox set it next to the other corks, then noticed there was a horizontal crack that ringed the cork. She ran her fingernail along the crack and the cork opened to reveal a thumb drive.

Proof.

She swept the kitchen stuff back in the drawer and let herself out, her nerves zinging. This was what she'd been working for. The shitty people she interviewed, the resistance, the threats, it all came down to a wine cork. She locked up the apartment and ran down the stairs, headlong into John Holt, the creepy neighbor from the main floor.

His mouth opened to greet her.

"Got to go," she told him. She ran through the lobby door before he could call to her. Wahoo! She hopped over the food wrappers, a black plastic garbage bag, and an empty pint of Jim Beam the homeless guys had left behind, skipped through the rain to her truck, and climbed in. Her fingers trembled around the cork, but she got the thumb drive slotted into the laptop.

Here it was: proof Hadley was blackmailing or threatening Slocum—jumpy video of Slocum's examining room, cash exchanged for a written prescription, and the date printed at the bottom of each exchange. Hadley started up this practice three years ago. Lennox could verify the dates, but it seemed it all began around the date that she was dumped by Slocum.

Lennox started the Bronco. A good bottle of Cabernet and a night off was in order. She got a call from Fish.

"I don't know how to tell you this," he said.

She sighed, sick to death of coaxing people to communicate. "Just put your lips together and speak."

"You're not that into Shawn, right?"

"No. Fish. I found the murderer."

"Who?" Fish's voice was wary.

"Dr. James Slocum. I told you it wasn't Jagoda."

"Where are you?" He sounded panicked.

"I'm headed home."

"I'll meet you there. Don't talk to anyone. Not Kline. No one. Cooper, promise me."

"What is wrong with you?"

"Promise me." He nearly broke her eardrum.

She told him fine, fine—don't get his boxers in a twist, she'd see him at her house.

. . .

Fish was waiting at the curb. He hopped out of his car.

"We've got to talk." Fish, who'd never touched her in his life, had her by the elbow and was leading her up the porch steps.

"What is wrong with you?" she said.

He told her to shut up and get inside.

She told Fish to sit down, for Chrissake, and tell her what his problem was.

"Slocum didn't murder Hadley Eberhart. He was up on Mt. Hood with his wife."

"The desk clerk signed a statement that he left after ten and didn't get back to the lodge until 4am."

"We had a tail on him," Fish said. "He was at the Ratskeller in Government Camp. Then he went off with a skank until 3:30."

"I've got proof Hadley was blackmailing him."

"About what?"

"Running a pill mill. Hadley took videos and backed them up on a drive."

"Great. Hand it over." Fish leaned forward with his hand outstretched.

"I'm not giving you shit," she said. "I've slaved to get this proof. I'm taking it to Kline."

He gave a quick shake of his head, a flash of sympathy that hardened fast into cop-mode. "What do you have proof of?" he said.

"I told you. Blackmail. Hadley called Slocum the night of her murder. Demanded drugs. He drove down the mountain and drowned her ass."

"You're wrong. I need the video. Look," he said. "We've been tracking this guy for nine months and we're about to bust him on multiple charges: conspiring to sell Oxycodone, health care fraud, money laundering. And we don't need you fucking it up."

"He murdered Hadley."

Fish's voice grew louder. "He's being watched every minute. Day and night. You were up there yesterday and succeeded in pissing off his wife."

The older guy working as a paid thug. "The ex-cop," she said.

"Not really an ex." He wiggled his fingers. "Give me the video."

She dragged herself out of the chair and retrieved the thumb drive. Forget the bottle of Cabernet, Lennox wanted to climb into bed and stay there forever.

"Wow." Fish rubbed the cork drive with his thumb. "Clever."

"If you're through, I've got a lot to do."

"Yeah. Sure," he said. "So, you get that you have to drop this thing with Slocum or you'll blow our investigation."

"Yeah. I get it. Too bad you didn't call before I went to all that work."

"Shit. Well." He heaved a sigh. "Guess I'm the bearer of bad news today. So, you're not that into Shawn, right?"

"I already told you. Why? Is he seeing someone?"

"That's the thing. I did see him with a woman. You'll never guess."

She groaned. "Don't make me guess."

"Jill Rykoff."

A flutter of hope brushed against the wet cement that was her life. Shawn and Jill? It was so insanely unlikely, but if true, it meant that Jill and Kline were not a thing. What? Now she was happy that maybe Kline was available? What was wrong with her, was she going mental?

"They were probably just shooting the shit," she said. "They do know each other."

"Naw. You and I shoot the shit. You don't rub your bare foot against my leg while you're talking to me."

"That's weird. You think they're a thing or something?"

"Beats me," Fish said. "I just figured you'd want to know. You're okay with it, right?"

Why in the world would a prosecutor play footsie with a patrolman? Shawn was a cutie, but Jill was fifty-two levels above him in status.

The bigger question was why Lennox kept seeing Shawn here, there, and everywhere.

CHAPTER 29

Whoever murdered Hadley had to know that she was at Ito's that night. With Slocum out of the running, that left Lennox with Terry Purcell. But who the fuck was he? And how did he get a cop to engineer Tomek's release?

After Fish left, Lennox called Shawn and tried to coax him into a having a drink with her. He was reluctant. There was a manhunt going on, didn't she know? "What kind of an Irishman are you, you'd turn down a drink?"

"Fine," he told her.

"Five?" she said.

"Why so early?" he said. She told him she was working nights. "You still flogging the Jagoda case?" Ha ha.

Was he the dirty cop? The guy she saw driving up to the Slocums in a black and white? They agreed to meet at the Alameda Brew Pub at five the following day.

Lennox ran the last batch of license plate numbers: eleven of them and still nothing she could connect to Hadley or to Terry Purcell.

Still flogging the Jagoda case. Lennox followed Pieter from his house to a bar called *Lush* in North Portland. Every night he drove to a different bar, but it was the same deal: one-story building, wood-sided, flat-roofed, no windows. Lennox had seen plenty of bars exactly like these and partaken of their wares, dive bars being a hobby she shared with an ex-boyfriend. She was so over it.

She sipped from a bottle of water and watched Pieter's Mercedes, which was parked in the darkest corner of the parking lot away from the security light mounted on the back corner of the building. A mix of people, fat and skinny, young and gray-haired, drove into the parking lot and walked over to Pieter's car. Lennox jotted down their license plate numbers.

Yup, still flogging the case.

Tomek was still in the ICU, needing two more surgeries to repair his gut where the tissue tore from the stitches. More intestine removed. Crisis, then things would settle back into a state of high worry. Idzi no longer bothered to dress up or moisturize. She was wearing the same old shapeless black tunic over knit pants the last three times Lennox had seen her. Her hair looked unwashed. What would the old lady do if Tomek didn't survive this? You could read that thought on her face.

A slow fifteen minutes crawled by, then Lennox heard the unmistakable grumble of a flock of Harleys. Five bikes swung into the parking lot. Lennox rolled her window down partway, hoping to catch what they said to each other. She used her field glasses to read all their license numbers. Pieter climbed out of his car and leaned against the front fender, watching the bikers park and walk over to him.

The lead guy, short but powerfully built, approached Pieter and tried to clap him on the back. Pieter batted his hand away. They had words, but Lennox couldn't hear anything that was said. The biker shoved Pieter in the chest. Pieter shoved him back. The biker pulled something from his pocket. Pieter pulled out a knife. Their blades flashed in the security light. The men circled around Pieter. Pieter swiped at the leader. And missed.

Lennox called 911. Bikers trying to kill a civilian, she told them. Then one of the other bikers pushed Pieter from behind. Pieter stumbled and the lead man knifed Pieter in the chest.

Pieter fell to his knees. The bikers took turns kicking him. Pieter tipped to his left side and curled up, one arm protecting his head. She was watching a potential murder, and she had no backup. If she interfered, she'd blow her cover. And cover was all she had going at this point. If this surveillance didn't work, she had no other play. Meanwhile the bikers were in the process of caving Pieter's ribs in. She grabbed Old Ugly from her leg holster and jumped from her car.

"Hands up. Now!" she shouted. They stopped kicking, but the lead biker guy patted down Pieter, presumably looking for dope. "Now!" she repeated. When he didn't react, she figured it was her girly voice, a female not worthy of these tough guys' respect. So she aimed at a Harley and shot. The bullet pinged off something. Hard to say what part of the bike it was in the low light.

Never had she heard such a chorus of swearing in her life. And given her life, that was saying something. One of the bikers threw his hands in the air. "Don't shoot, lady."

"Hands up, or another Harley gets it," she said.

The other four put their hands in the air.

"I've called the cops. You've got four minutes, tops, before they show up."

The men rushed to their bikes and started them up. The lead bike sputtered but caught. They left in a roar of exhaust, each of them giving her the one-finger salute as they pulled onto Lombard Street.

Pieter was lying on his side in the dim light. She knelt next to him as he squinted up at her. She saw the dark seep of a wound in his shoulder. "Can you move?"

"You."

"Like a bad penny. The cops will be here in about two minutes. Can I get you out of here?"

"Yeah." He struggled to his knees and swore something in Polish under his breath.

"Should we wait for an ambulance?"

"No."

She helped him to his feet and over to his Mercedes. He wanted to drive. "We don't have time to argue," she said. She eased him into the passenger side as much as she could ease a guy who weighed a hundred pounds more than her. He groaned as he reached in his pocket and handed her the keys. The sirens could be heard from a half-mile away.

Lush's sign was still in her rear window when the patrol cars went screaming past.

She glanced at Pieter. His face was twisted in pain. She handed him her cap. Told him to press it against his shoulder. "I'll get you to the hospital."

"No. Just get me to Ma's."

"I know about this shit. Torn blood vessels, nerve damage, joint damage. It's nothing to fuck with."

He swore under his breath.

"Why didn't you come armed?"

He shook his head violently, then gasped in pain.

He never did give her an answer. His brother was shot four days ago. Why didn't he carry a gun? She white-knuckle drove, keeping the car within the speed limit, wanting to go faster but not daring to get stopped by the law.

Pieter shivered and then started trembling.

"Stay with me," she said.

He passed out. She pulled to the curb. Unlocked the trunk of the Mercedes and looked for a car blanket, bungee cords, anything she could use to hold a bandage against his wound. She found a roll of duct tape. Went to his side of the car and unbuckled his seatbelt. He flopped to his side. She checked his back pockets and found his wallet, tossed it on the floor. His jacket, his hoody, everything was soaked in blood. She shimmied out of her sweater. Duct taped the sweater around his shoulder and to his chest. She checked his jacket pockets for drugs. The biker dude had cleaned him out.

He was still unconscious and she needed him conscious. He was going into shock. If his blood pressure crashed, his heart would stop. "Wake up," she yelled. He groaned. She slapped his face.

"Awww."

She slapped him again. "We're headed for ER," she shouted.

Fifteen minutes passed that felt like an hour before she pulled into the circular driveway at the Emanuel ER. In no time, Pieter went from a wheelchair to a gurney headed for surgery.

"Are you hurt?" the admittance nurse asked Lennox.

Lennox looked down at herself. She was covered in blood. She explained that it was the man's blood. She had found him on the side of the road on her way home. She had no idea who he was.

Lennox called Idzi. Told her Pieter had been hurt and was at Emanuel.

Idzi started moaning.

"Do you have someone to watch Tomek?"

The old lady didn't answer.

"You stay with Tomek," Lennox said. "I'll stay here until Pieter comes out of surgery. Tomorrow I'll round up some friends. People we can trust to help you watch Tomek."

CHAPTER 30

A young woman walked into the hospital restroom while Lennox was blotting the blood off her leather jacket. The floor was littered with wet, bloody paper towels. The woman's eyes grew round. "I'm fine," Lennox told her. Apparently, the fact that she was fine alarmed the woman even more. "I'll use another one," the woman said and backed out of the room.

After Lennox cleaned up as best she could, she settled in the corner of the waiting room and called Ham.

"What time is it?"

She apologized for the late hour and told him she was at the hospital, that Pieter had been stabbed. Ham groaned. "The Jagodas. You woke me to tell me that?" She told him that she'd make a deal with him, she'd take him off phone detail if he gathered the gang together tomorrow night, and not to tell them what it was about. "What is it about?" Ham said. "I wouldn't ask if I didn't really need all of you. Please," she said.

The surgeon met Lennox in the waiting room an hour

later. Pieter was in recovery, doing fine, the doc told her. In four months, he'd have full use of his arm. She read her phone and waited until the nursing staff wheeled Pieter into his room.

"You," he said when he saw Lennox, then fell asleep.

Lennox left for home. It was two in the morning before she and Gretchen climbed the stairs to bed.

• • •

The guys were gathered around the poker table the next night. Their concerned faces looked up from fish platters. A spot of tartar sauce was lost in Ham's beard.

"This better not be about the Jagoda case," Fish said. His thick hair looked like a small brown animal was balanced on his head. "Ham said it was an emergency."

"Are you okay?" Jerry leaned forward, the top button unbuttoned on his dress shirt, his tie loosened.

"I need your help," she said. "You all know that someone hacked the jail computers and Tomek was freed and then shot."

Fish groaned. "No one cares, Cooper."

He had nerve. First it was stay away from the Slocums, now no one cares if Tomek lives or dies. "What the hell is wrong with you? It was one of your police brethren that let Jagoda out in the first place. Maybe one of them shot Tomek as well."

Fish threw up his hands.

A chorus of "Hold on, hold on."

"I don't get why you're defending this guy." Fish was red in the face, and she knew she was red too.

"Did I not cooperate with you?" Lennox said. "I didn't have to."

"Yes, you do have to cooperate with me. I'm not in the private sector," Fish said through gritted teeth.

Fish would still be working patrol if it weren't for Lennox. He was dandy so long as there was something in it for him, but you didn't have to scratch too deep to find the inner jerk. "Yeah, well maybe you got your information from a dirty cop," she said.

"That's it. I'm out of here." Fish slapped a couple bills on the table and slammed out the door.

"Someone's dirty." Lennox looked around the table. 2-K swallowed. Sarge's bald head was red as a clown's nose. "You know that, right?"

"Let's everyone take a breath here," Jerry said, using his best arbitrator voice.

Lennox was so pissed, so tired, so alone, she had trouble holding it together. She gulped down her Jack and Coke, counted her breaths. When she looked up from the table, she saw all the guys watching her.

"Let's hear her out," Jerry said.

"You all know that the so-called computer glitch wasn't a glitch, right?"

The guys' reaction fell into two camps: cops on one side, lawyer and accountant on the other. The cops shrugged; the others nodded.

"Tomek isn't safe. Anyone can come into his room posing as a doctor or a relative. It would take nothing to finish him off."

"But he has a police guard," Sarge said.

"The police guard is there to keep Tomek from escaping police custody." That was granting Sarge the fairy tale that the entire Portland Police Bureau was honest and true, which was a load of crap. What was wrong with him that he couldn't admit that?

"What do you need?" Jerry said.

"Tomek needs twenty-four hours a day guarding. I do what I can, but as of now, the trial's going forward. I need help." She swallowed. "I don't know who else can help me other than you guys." She looked around the table.

"Give me a day to set it up. Clear it with Meghan," Ham said.

"I can pull some vacation," Jerry said. "Help with day shifts."

"No. I'm sorry," Sarge said. "Those people are bad. If they're in trouble now, it's because of what they do for a living. This is a wrong cause you've taken up, Lennox." He stood up and walked around the table, squeezed her shoulder. "I'm sorry." Sarge left the room.

That left the last cop: 2-K. He quickly picked up his beer glass and chugged the remaining beer. She watched his Adam's apple move up and down. He put the empty pint on the table, then realized that everyone was waiting for him to speak. He tipped his head towards one shoulder then the next. "You've got a point."

"So?" she said. Jerry and Ham leaned forward.

"Yeah. I can pitch in."

CHAPTER 31

Lennox couldn't get it out of her mind, wondering what the connection between Jill and Shawn could possibly be. Wondering if Shawn could be the dirty cop. But even if Lennox took Shawn to bed, the minute she brought up Jill, he'd know she was interviewing him.

A giant bronze hop flower hung from the brick-faced two-story on the north side of Fremont. It was bright and shiny in a row of new bright and shiny businesses. Lennox remembered the lumberyard and some kind of textile factory that used to be there. Stanich's, a bar famous for its hamburgers and fries since the sixties, still anchored the corner, but the rest of the buildings had been demolished to make way for hot yoga, a hair salon, a children's bookstore, a boutique gym, and of course the Alameda Brewhouse. Now everyone called Fremont Street from 49th Avenue to 35th the Beaumont Village.

It was five in the afternoon and already full on night. All the businesses were lined and lit by tiny white Christmas lights. Lennox parked and entered the bar. The lovely smell of boiling malt and hops wafted from giant stainless steel brewing kettles. Shawn was in a middle booth. The room was high-ceilinged and dim, but even in the lamp light Lennox could tell that he had recently shaved. He wore a fresh shirt and jeans, his copper-colored hair still wet from the shower.

"I see you found some company." She nodded towards the empty shot glass and half-drunk pint. He aimed a crooked Irish grin at her, his face open, waiting to see where the night was headed. But he remained seated. Lennox remembered him being rather courtly in an ironic sort of way. Could he really have hooked up with Jill?

"What's up?" he said.

She gave him her version of flirty: one shoulder forward, looking up at him through her eyelashes, leaning towards him, her arms on the table. "You know, just checking in. Haven't seen you in a while. Like you said on the phone, the manhunt, right? How's that going?"

His grin twisted from cute to wry. "You know I can't discuss that with you. How's the Jagoda case going?"

"You know I can't discuss that with you," she said. "So what are we going to talk about?"

He shook his head. "I don't know. You're the one who called me."

He craned his neck in all directions, casting about for their waiter. Shawn motioned that he had a companion, then settled back to look at Lennox again.

The waiter swung by. Took her order for Jack and Coke and another shot and beer for Shawn. Lennox asked him if he was hungry.

"Why not?" Shawn said. "You want to share a burger and fries?"

She nodded and smiled, but she wasn't fooling him. If they had a three-course dinner with wine and candlelight, she wasn't going to convince him they were having a date. She had shut him down too many times. And it was a shame. His freckles, his lovely nose, perfect white teeth. He was a nice Irish cop and interesting enough.

She asked him what he'd been up to.

His partner had finally transferred to a desk after a year of grousing about his feet. Shawn had been to a couple of Ducks games in Eugene.

The waiter brought their drinks.

"Seeing anyone?" she said.

He straightened his spine against the back of the booth. "Now, why would you ask that?" He wasn't stupid.

She took a mouthful of Jack and Coke and swallowed. "It's not like I don't care."

"Do you care?" He stared at her like a seasoned detective, watching for any lying twitch on her face.

She shrugged and looked down at her cocktail. "I've been working hard. Like you said, flogging the Jagoda case."

"Yeah, I've been working hard, too."

They both sipped their drinks. She looked at the other people in the place. The family sitting next to them at a table: two little pre-school girls, one in tights and a long sweater, the other in a pale lavender fairy princess outfit. The kids' parents were still in their twenties.

Lennox was sitting across the table from a very cute man who she could be dating. Instead she was trying to fox him into telling her about Jill.

He picked up his drink. "Look, I saw your friend. The hairy one, okay? He was giving me the stink eye the other night when I was with Jill."

"You got to admit, it looks odd."

He shrugged. She'd insulted him. "Some say I have appeal."

"You do. Absolutely," she said. "But Rykoff? She's a lawyer. You and me work for them. We're the foot soldiers and the lawyers are never going to think of us as anything else." It's what Lennox believed, but it felt bad to say it out loud.

The waiter brought their food.

Shawn picked up a fry. "It was nothing. She bought me a couple drinks."

"What did you talk about?"

He leaned back in his chair. "Is that what this is about?" he said. "The two of you. No wonder you wouldn't sleep with me."

"Excuse me?" Lennox wished he'd tell her because she had no idea what was going on.

Shawn snorted. "That bullshit about lawyers and soldiers. You two are hot for each other. Somehow I got in the middle of that."

"What the fuck are you talking about?"

"She buys me drinks. Asks me about you. You buy me drinks, ask me about her. I feel like I'm back in high school." He dug in his back pocket for his wallet and slapped money on the table. "All I can say is good luck. She's a handful."

He thought Lennox was a lesbian? Is that how she came off? "Wait. Wait!" Lennox grabbed the sleeve of his jacket. "It's complicated," she said. It was a meaningless thing to say. Everything was complicated. She started again. "I'm in love with someone, but he doesn't love me." There, she'd said it out loud. She thought it was true. She took a long pull from her drink to keep from howling.

Shawn stared at her. "He?"

She shook her head. "Not Jill."

He relaxed back into the booth.

"I'm sorry," she said. She slid his money towards him.

They sat across from one another, not talking. The hamburger and fries getting colder by the minute.

"I got to get back to the hospital. Can I ask you one last question?"

He gave his head a slight nod.

"What did you mean when you said Jill was a handful?"

"When I saw her, she was a little wound up."

He looked a little squirmy, a little embarrassed. Lennox leaned forward. "Wound up?"

"She said she'd caught a head cold. The medicine made her loopy."

"You say that like you don't believe it."

"I'm not stupid."

"Are you saying she was high?"

He nodded, gave her a crooked smile.

"Coke?" she said.

He shrugged. "How do I know? I'm just a foot soldier."

• • •

Shawn walked her to her truck.

"See you soon," she said.

"Sure," he said with no conviction. He crossed the street and walked away.

Lennox started the truck and caught 47th headed towards Providence Hospital. Her wipers scraped across her windshield. She turned on the radio.

The news was all about the two violent felons who

were still at large. "Keep your doors locked; be aware of your surroundings when you enter or exit your car. A third fugitive not yet back in prison, Tomek Jagoda, charged with homicide, is still hospitalized in critical condition," the newswoman said.

The case was making her crazy. She pushed the button for classic rock and heard Foreigner's "I Wanna Know What Love Is." She turned the radio off. She was stupid having feelings for Kline when Shawn was right there. Her taste in men…she was like her dad, going for the wrong person…

The truck was cold and smelled like wet dog. Lennox remembered seeing Jill at Higgins, flirting with the attorneys from the DA. She was high, not drunk. All the years she spent in this business, she knew the difference. Lawyers were infamous for doing coke. How else were they able to keep up with the hours they worked and the amount of data they needed to process? And it wasn't as if they could go to a special boutique to buy the stuff.

Drugs were the connection between Hadley's murder and Tomek's shooting.

CHAPTER 32

Lennox rode the elevator to the fourth floor at the hospital. A nurse in purple scrubs wearing a face mask wheeled an old lady over to the staff elevator and pressed the button. "Room 412. Code blue," a calm voice said over the intercom. Room 412—Tomek's room. Two other nurses sprinted past Lennox and headed for the ICU.

"Excuse me," a shaky voice said from behind Lennox. Lennox was already trotting towards Tomek's room thinking Tomek's heart had given out, thinking septic shock, another bleed. "Help," the old voice called.

Shit! Lennox half-turned and saw the same old lady in the wheelchair facing a wall next to the staff elevator, but the nurse was gone.

"Code blue. Room 412." Another nurse sprinted past.

Lennox pushed the old woman's chair to the ICU nurses' station. It was abandoned. An alarm was beeping from Tomek's room. A red light was blinking over the empty station. Tomek's room was crowded with hospital staff.

The alarm kept beeping.

"Excuse me," the old lady said.

"I'm not a nurse. Okay?" Lennox said, speaking louder than she intended. "Someone will come along soon to help you."

That damn alarm was beeping still. It was freaking her out. What the hell were they doing in there?

Lennox paced the floor, hoping he wasn't dead and steeling herself for the possibility. Where the hell was Ham? He was supposed to be guarding Tomek. Where the hell was the police guard?

Lennox phoned Idzi. The old woman sounded half asleep. Lennox told her Tomek was in trouble. "Where's Albin?" Idzi said. Her old man. Lennox had no idea.

A nurse hustled out of Tomek's room.

"Excuse me," Lennox said. The nurse kept walking. Lennox jogged ahead of her. She raised her voice. "My brother. Is he okay? Tomek Jagoda."

"He's still alive." The nurse wore a lanyard with her photo ID on a laminated card. Lennox tried to ask the nurse more questions, but was told she had to go to the waiting room.

Like hell Lennox was going anywhere. She walked back to the nurses' desk and waited. The nurses and CNAs slowly trickled out of Tomek's room. They deflected any of Lennox's questions: *Was he all right? What happened?*

Lennox found old man Jagoda—tiny, bent, with a great mane of hair. He was wandering down the corridor, his fly unzipped.

"Mr. Jagoda? Do you remember me?"

"Uhh." He waved a veiny hand in front of his face.

"Can you hear me?" she pitched her voice twice as loud. He squinted his eyes and did the hand wave thing.

Maybe he was deaf, maybe he only spoke Polish. One thing was for sure, a stick of furniture would do just as good a job of guarding Tomek.

At last, Dr. Lee came out of Tomek's room. Lennox identified herself.

"What happened?" she said.

"Your brother pulled out his breathing tube," the doctor told her. "He's not ready to breathe on his own."

"But, I don't understand," she said. "Had he regained consciousness?"

The doctor tipped his head. "This happens. The breathing tube is uncomfortable; the patient is disoriented."

"So he regained consciousness?" Lennox insisted.

The doctor actually made eye contact. "That's what we assume."

He told her that Tomek had done some damage to his larynx, but that it was likely to heal. There might be a slight chance of brain damage from oxygen deprivation. "We'll have to wait and see." Brain damage. She'd let Tomek down. She couldn't keep anyone safe. They all died. Her vision tunneled. There was a buzzing in her ears. She had to sit.

"Are you all right?" the doctor said in a faraway voice. Someone helped her to a chair and told her to keep her head between her knees.

"Take it easy," Dr. Lee said.

Slowly, her vision came back.

"I'm sorry," she told them. "I'm fine now."

"Slowly," they told her. A nurse handed her a glass of water. It was humiliating. She'd never come this close to fainting in her life. She'd been knocked unconscious; this was different. At last, she assured them she could stand. Where the hell was Ham? The cop charged with watching him?

Eventually she was able to ask the duty nurse more questions. Had she seen any visitors? Just Tomek's father. Had she noticed a doctor or some other nurse, a CNA who had checked in with Tomek shortly before the alarms went off? Mandy, Tomek's CNA, had checked Tomek's vitals a half hour before. "Was he conscious?" Lennox said.

"He must have been," the nurse said.

"Could you ask Mandy? Where's his guard?"

The nurse looked at a clipboard. "Deputy Jason Shepherd. Maybe in the cafeteria?"

The cafeteria was nearly empty. A few shell-shocked families sat, heads together. The deputy supposedly guarding Tomek was drinking coffee at a table for four. Lennox told him she was on Jagoda's defense team. She showed him her license.

The deputy looked at her with half-closed eyes. "Am I supposed to be impressed?"

He was in his late twenties, white, skinny, and bored. A paperback with a bent cover sat next to his coffee cup.

It was all she could do to control herself. She'd lost patience with these fuckers. They could arrest her; she didn't give a shit. She wanted answers.

"Your name, officer."

"Deputy Jason Shepherd."

He lifted a shoulder, a bored look on his face.

"What happened upstairs?"

"You mean Jagoda?"

The idiot. One minute into the conversation she wanted to shake him.

"Yeah. What happened?"

"The alarms went off. Nurses came running. He's gut-shot. Most times they don't make it."

Not a shred of pity. The guy felt less emotion for Tomek than she did for a dead squirrel in the middle of the street.

"Who came in Jagoda's room before the alarms started ringing?"

"A nurse. Or doctor. I can't tell them apart."

"Male? Female?"

"Male, I guess."

"Are you going to make me play twenty questions with you?"

"Lady, I'm not here to answer your questions."

"You're here to make sure Tomek doesn't try to leave his room. Am I right?"

He nodded.

"So how do you know that the nurse or doctor you saw wasn't Tomek dressed in scrubs?"

He swallowed more coffee, ignoring her.

"I'm going to stay here all night like a mosquito."

"A mosquito can be swatted."

Lennox leaned forward, halfway across the table, her teeth bared in his face. She wanted to hit him so bad. "Try it, asshole."

He straightened in his seat. Did a slow neck roll just to let her know she wasn't getting to him. "Too skinny," he said.

"What did he look like?"

"I don't know. Tall. Purple scrubs. Hair under a cap. Mask." The cop shrugged. "Everybody around here pretty much looks the same."

Purple scrubs. The guy who'd passed Lennox at the elevators wore purple scrubs. There was something about that guy...

Lennox tried to remember her impression of the nurse who'd taken the staff elevator. He'd been six-foot, wearing a surgery mask. What else? No lanyard with ID. What else? She remembered he smelled good. After shave, cologne. Something. Weird for a health care person to wear perfume.

"Did you notice if he smelled like anything?"

"Are you kidding me?" The cop rolled his eyes. "The guy probably had nothing to do with Jagoda's problems. Like I said, most times these people don't make it."

CHAPTER 33

Ten at night. She sat next to Tomek's bed, and listened to the blips and hiss of the medical machinery keeping Tomek alive. At no time did he stir. Not a twitch. Idzi and Pieter were late getting to the hospital.

Ham walked into Tomek's room looking wrinkled and tired.

"I'm sorry Coop, I got here at six, like I said I would, and the old lady told me they had it covered."

"Fuck," she said.

"What happened?"

"Someone came in here past the guard and tried to kill Tomek. The only one watching out for him was his ancient father."

"I'm sorry," Ham said.

She told him it wasn't his fault. Then a call came in from Kline.

"How's our client?" Kline said.

She told him about the newest crisis.

"Is he going to make it?"

Lennox thought there was some concern in his voice. "The doctor says there was a slight chance of brain damage."

Kline took a deep breath. "Okay."

She knew he was weighing next moves. It wasn't a good time to tell him her theories. She heard Ham on his phone telling Meghan he wasn't coming home tonight.

"Rykoff has scheduled a meeting with the judge to discuss the plea," Kline said. That was the reason he called. Back to business. If she wanted anything more out of him, she was going to have to ask.

"Why? Didn't you tell Rykoff?"

"I haven't been able to get a hold of her. The hearing's at nine. I want you there."

"But—" Lennox was thinking of Tomek—of who was guarding him and who was trying to kill him.

"No," Kline said. "This shit storm of a case is your doing. I want you there when the judge lands on us with both feet."

"Someone came into the hospital tonight and tried to murder Tomek."

"Your family's here," Tomek's nurse told Lennox.

"I've got to go. I'll see you tomorrow."

Ham had settled in next to Tomek's bed. If he was surprised that Lennox's "family" was waiting for her, he didn't show it. Lennox woke up old man Jagoda and led him, in slow shuffling steps, down the shiny corridor to the waiting room.

The TV was turned to Fox News, the sound a low buzz. The room was empty except Pieter and Idzi sitting together on the purple sofa under the photo of Mt. Hood. It was hard to know who looked worse: Idzi with her puffy eyes and wrinkles, or Pieter, his skin pale and waxy, his arm in a sling.

Lennox sat the old man down next to Idzi, who leaned over and shouted something in Polish. The old man shook his head. Idzi patted his knee and straightened the front of his sweater.

"How are you doing?" Lennox asked Pieter.

He scowled and gave his head a slight shake, then winced in pain.

All the worry, all the effort, turned to anger.

"I saved your life, you asshole," she said to Pieter. "I not only saved your life, but I kept you out of jail. I've been busting my hump for you people. For what?"

Pieter refused to make eye contact. Idzi blinked.

"There was an attempt on Tomek's life tonight." Lennox let that sink in.

The old woman looked hollowed out. Like everything she'd hoped for in her life had evaporated. "What happened?" she whispered.

"Near as I can make out, someone dressed in scrubs and a surgical mask walked past the guard and pulled Tomek's air tube out. Hard to know whether Tomek did any breathing on his own before the nursing staff reinserted the tube."

Idzi started to cry softly. Pieter sat there like a rock, his jaw clamped down hard.

"I don't give a shit whether your family deals drugs or not. Either you start to work with me, or who ever tried to off Tomek will come back and finish the job."

"What do you want from us?" Idzi's voice was so soft, Lennox could hardly hear it over the TV buzz.

"Hadley made two calls to Terry Purcell the night of

her murder. But there is no Terry Purcell in Oregon, and the two calls were made to a burner phone. He was Tomek's client. Who is he?"

Idzi looked at Pieter. Nodded to him.

"How do I know you're not wearing a wire?" he said.

"Come on, Idzi. We'll go in the bathroom, you can check me out."

Lennox had pulled the sweater over her head before the door completely closed. It was a large square of a room with a shiny vinyl floor, a sink, and a toilet with handicap rails. The overhead light made Idzi's skin look like yellow crepe. Lennox didn't look so hot either.

"Okay?"

Idzi's eyes followed the jagged scar that ran down Lennox's side. She nodded. Lennox put her sweater back on. Pulled off her cowboy boots. Handed them, one by one to Idzi. The old lady stood there dumbly, a boot under each arm.

"Pieter has trust issues," Idzi said.

He was a dealer. Of course he had trust issues. It probably hadn't helped that Lennox hit him hard with a can of pepper spray. Lennox had been pepper sprayed once. She'd rather be shot. Lennox unzipped her jeans and stepped out of them.

The old woman glanced at Lennox's scar that continued along her flank to her knee. "Okay. Okay," the old woman muttered.

Lennox was the one standing in her underwear, and the old woman was embarrassed. Lennox pulled up her pants. They returned to the waiting room.

Both Pieter and his father snoozed on the sofa. Pieter's

head was thrown back, breathing through his mouth. His head rocked forward. He snorted, but he didn't wake up.

"You've got to let me help you with guarding Tomek," Lennox said. "Your husband is too old to be of any use here."

Idzi nodded again. The sparky old lady who broke into Lennox's house a month ago was beaten. It was as if Tomek had stolen her heart.

"Pieter," Idzi said. She said something in Polish and shook his knee. Pieter roused and groaned. If Lennox didn't dislike the guy so much, she'd feel sorry for him.

"No wire," Idzi told her son.

Lennox pulled a chair so that it faced the sofa. She sat knee to knee with Pieter. Mints floated on top of his cigarette breath. His shave was a little sketchy. His right shoulder must be giving him hell.

"Terry Purcell," Lennox said. "I've called his number, the one I had from a month ago. It's dead."

"I don't know about any other number." Pieter shook his head. "He was Tomek's guy until Tomek went away. He buys coke once in a while, a speedball. You know what that is?"

"Yeah. Cocaine cut with heroin," Lennox said. "Tomek's thumbprint was on a packet with traces of speedball at Hadley's crime scene. What does Terry look like? How often does he buy?"

Pieter said something to Idzi in Polish. She pinched his arm.

"Damn," he said.

"Go on," the old woman told him.

"He comes around once a week most times."

"What does he look like? C'mon, don't make me drag this shit out of you."

Old man Jagoda sat upright with a snort.

"He's—I don't know. He's queer. I don't like to look at him."

"How tall? Fat? Skinny?"

"Six foot. Skinnier than me. He always wears a knit cap over his head pulled down to his eyebrows. Parka. Work boots."

Idzi asked him something in Polish. They talked back and forth. Lennox didn't understand a word.

"Tomorrow night," he said. "Terry's supposed to meet me at Lulu's at seven."

"What kind of a car does he drive?"

"He doesn't. He comes out from the bar."

Lennox told them she could get friends to watch Tomek tomorrow. She told Idzi to get some rest.

"Don't look for me," she told Pieter. "And when you see Terry, act normal. I'll call you after."

CHAPTER 34

Lennox arrived at security in her court clothes: charcoal suit and a turquoise silk blouse, kitten heels that pinched her feet, a raincoat over her arm. The courthouse halls smelled of a hundred years of furniture polish and decaying plaster. Lennox climbed the stairs past a stream of cops, attorneys, and the accused to Room 233, the bottom half of an original two-story courtroom. It looked very sixties—paneled in honey-colored wood, acoustic tile on the low ceiling.

At the back of the courtroom, five attorneys sat shoulder to shoulder with five sorry-looking clients. At the front of the courtroom, the clerk, a narrow-shouldered man, dropped a stack of paper at his desk and left the room. The court reporter fiddled with her stenotype. Kline sat all alone at the attorney desk on the defense side of the aisle. Across the aisle, the prosecuting table was empty. Where were they?

Kline turned to see who had just come in and seemed disappointed that it was little old her. He looked scrubbed but weary, his suit impeccable as ever.

She plopped her briefcase next to her chair and leaned forward across the bar, got a whiff of his clean scent. He always smelled so wonderfully clean. "Did you get a hold of Rykoff?" she said in a low voice. Courtrooms were like churches that way. You never spoke up unless you were talking to the judge, who basically stood in for God in the halls of justice.

Kline shook his head.

Lennox wanted to ask where the hell Rykoff was, but didn't. Instead, she asked who they drew for a judge.

Janet Thomas.

"I'm not familiar," Lennox said. "What's she like?"

"Fair. A little severe. How's Jagoda? Any sense of when he'll recover?"

The clerk reentered the courtroom. "All rise. The Honorable Judge Thomas presiding."

Lennox and Kline jumped to their feet just as Judge Thomas walked briskly into the room, her black bob swinging, a smile on her face like she found life, on the whole, very satisfying.

The judge sat. Then they all sat. "Smith vs. Theroux?" the judge said.

The clerk bustled over to the bench and reshuffled the judge's paperwork. The judge's smile dropped.

Kline stood. "No, Judge. The State of Oregon vs. Tomek Jagoda."

Judge Thomas wrinkled her long thin nose at the attorney table, then turned to her clerk. "Who's missing?"

The clerk spoke up. "The prosecutor, your Honor. Jill Rykoff."

The judge poked her paperwork with a bony finger.

"Didn't her office ask for the hearing?" The good mood she'd walked in with was completely gone.

The clerk nodded.

"Where is she?" The judge glared at her clerk, who looked down at the stack of papers before him, then back to the judge.

"I'm not certain, Your Honor."

The courtroom door opened and Jill clattered up the aisle in a narrow skirt, lugging a bulging briefcase.

"I am so very sorry, Your Honor. A series of mishaps this morning—"

The judge waved a dismissive hand. "I don't want to hear your excuses, Counselor. Tell me, why am I here?"

"In the State of Oregon vs.—"

"Yes, yes. Go on."

"Mr. Kline and I have come to an agreement with Mr. Jagoda. He's changed his plea to guilty of a lesser charge."

The judge leaned forward. "Mr. Kline?"

Kline stood up. His ears, the twin mood rings of his persona, were deep red. "I think there's been a misunderstanding, Your Honor. I'm not authorized to change my client's plea at this time."

Rykoff jumped to her feet. "Wait a minute, Gus. I thought we had an understanding."

The court reporter's fingers flew over the keys. The clerk looked down at his feet. And the judge's once smiling mouth was pinched tight with irritation. She looked stonily first at Rykoff, then at Kline.

Kline cleared his throat. "You might know, Your Honor, that my client was hospitalized. He's still in a coma. We would like a short postponement of the trial until he's able to aid in his defense."

The judge summoned her clerk and looked over her calendar.

"How much time? Two weeks? Four weeks?"

"Your Honor, we really don't know."

The judge nodded. "We'll schedule another hearing in two weeks to see where we are."

She banged her gavel and leveled a blistering look at Rykoff. "I warn you, Counselor, don't waste my time again."

Rykoff hung her head. "Yes, Your Honor," she said in a meek little voice.

"What's next?" Judge Thomas asked her clerk.

Kline turned to walk out. Rykoff gathered her paperwork and strode after him. She was red in the face, her lips pulled back in a tight little snarl. Lennox followed, a foot soldier bringing up the rear.

The minute the courtroom door swung closed behind them, Jill grabbed Kline by the elbow and steered him further down the hall, away from the cluster of defendants and their attorneys. She towered over Kline in her heels. Lennox hung back, head down, ears peeled.

"What the fuck?" Jill said. "Why did you renege on the plea?" She acted like it was Kline's fault she got in dutch with the judge.

"I've tried to call you," Kline said.

"I've tried to call you," Jill said, mocking him, making him sound like a whiny little twit. Her nostrils were dilated, her mouth twisted in disdain. She was no longer beautiful, the way a dog isn't beautiful when it's bared its teeth at you. Kline saw that, Lennox knew he did. And it made her glad. For all her fabulousness, the goddess had feet of clay.

"This is all on you, Counselor," Kline said in a cold

voice. "Check in with the other side next time you schedule a hearing."

He turned and took the stairs, walking damn fast on those short legs of his. Jill shook her head, looking disgusted, then wiped her nose with her finger. It was a crude gesture for someone like Jill.

Of course.

Six-foot. Skinny. Liked her cocaine. Jill Rykoff could be the gay guy Tomek and Pieter sold drugs to. She could be the nurse in purple scrubs. She had the means to have drowned Hadley and to have sprung Tomek from jail and shot him.

Hadley Eberhart rode with Tomek from time to time while he made his deliveries in parking lots across East County. Hadley sees a guy—tall, thin, good looking, androgynous. Hadley recognizes that he or she could be trying to hide their identity. Then Hadley sees a photo of Jill Rykoff in the society page of the newspaper. Jill Rykoff, aka Terry Purcell. Hadley gets Terry Purcell's number from Tomek's phone and blackmails her for drugs.

Blackmail never ends happily. Hadley calls Terry the night she gets killed and threatens her. Jill agrees to meet her at Ito's place. A cinch to drown Hadley.

Lennox hustled down the marble steps to catch up with Kline. He was a block ahead of her, trotting through the rain, pedestrians parting for him like water. She'd have to jog in her damn kitten heels if she was going to catch up with him.

And then she stopped right in the middle of the sidewalk. People brushed past her. She took a deep breath. The air had a bite to it, but she didn't mind. Her feet hurt.

She was getting wet. Kline was madder than hell. And she hadn't felt this good for six long weeks.

Tonight Terry Purcell was going to buy coke from Pieter at Lulu's Bar. And Lennox would be there waiting for her. First she'd get a positive ID. The rest would come to Lennox.

A hot dog cart was parked under a big umbrella in front of the courthouse. Nothing says celebration like a foot long with mustard and extra kraut. Lennox gave the guy a big tip. She wasn't tired anymore. Things were shifting. She felt a certainty. *You know the murderer.*

CHAPTER 35

It was 6:30 at night. Street lights, the neon on storefronts, and a river of headlights from four lanes of traffic lit the MLK Boulevard. Lennox parked her rental car across the street from Lulu's parking lot in North Portland. The bar occupied the ground floor of an old brick hotel. The bar's name was tricked out in neon purple script over the door. This place was far more exposed than the other bars Lennox had followed Pieter to. The parking lot was small and faced the avenue, so Rykoff would have to park somewhere in the neighborhood and approach Pieter out in the open. That would make her edgier.

Rykoff had other reasons to be edgy. She'd flubbed her second attempt on Tomek's life, the plea hearing had gone badly, and she couldn't be sure that the Jagodas weren't on to her. If Tomek took the plea, if he was found guilty, if he died: any of those scenarios would turn the temperature down to tolerable.

Rykoff wasn't the only one who was edgy. The next twenty minutes were the slowest Lennox ever sat through.

She screwed the distance scope onto her surveillance camera and placed it alongside Old Ugly on the seat beside her. Her eyes and ears strained against the night. Her mind kept straying to all the ways to spin the story of Rykoff as Terry, all the glittering what-ifs.

She had to stay on task. This piece of surveillance was strictly to get some photos of Jill Rykoff posing as Terry Purcell and to tail her, if possible.

A Ram truck with monster wheels drove into Lulu's parking lot and stopped by Pieter's Mercedes. The truck's taillights haloed through Lennox's rain-beaded windshield. She rolled down her window and caught his license plate number, afraid to be caught taking a photo of Pieter and a customer just before Rykoff was due to arrive. Lennox watched the truck's driver approach Pieter's car. Pieter reached with his good hand, and they executed a clumsy handshake. The driver went back to his truck, reached overhead for the door handle, then climbed up his huge tire and swung back into the cab.

A white Subaru wagon pulled into the parking lot and two young guys went into the bar. Lennox slunk low in her seat and listened to the rain patter on the roof. Headlights blinded her as a truck pulled off MLK. A Land Rover. Jill's license plate. Lennox squeezed off three shots of the license plate. The truck kept moving down the street past Lulu's parking lot.

Rykoff.

Every hair on Lennox's body quivered. She pulled her gun closer to her thigh and picked up her camera. Rolled down her window and waited. A tall person in a parka and jeans walked down the sidewalk on Lennox's side of the street. Did Jill know that Lennox was waiting for her?

Lennox slid lower in her seat, slowly so as not to draw attention. Could Jill see her in the car? It seemed as if she were looking right at her. Lennox's mouth was dry; her tongue felt swollen. She couldn't swallow. She slowly raised the camera so that it cleared the dashboard and took two shots of Jill.

Abruptly, Jill crossed the street and walked over to Pieter's car. Lennox got two more shots of Jill making an exchange with Pieter. Jill turned and retreated back into the neighborhood. Lennox let her turn the corner before she started up the car, but by then Jill had disappeared.

• • •

Lennox got up early the next morning and constructed a photo array. She used pictures of both men and women: high cheekbones, blonde, beautiful, androgynous. Rykoff's photo was top row, second to the right.

Lennox drove up to Pieter's house at eleven in the morning. He answered the door in gray sweats, his arm still in a sling. His face was shadowed in beard; his eyes were bleary with sleep. He let her enter his living room, pointed for her to sit on the brown leather sofa. A half-empty coffee mug that said *World's Greatest Mom* sat on a glass and chrome coffee table. There were a couple of arm chairs, a very large television screen, and framed school pictures of his children on the wall.

"I know who the real Terry Purcell is," she said.

She showed him the picture of Jill that she took at Lulu's—Jill walking up to his wife's Mercedes. He wiped the sleep from his eyes, looked at the photo, slid it off the table, and balled it up with his good hand.

"Ma was wrong about you," he said, his voice weary. "You're setting us up."

"I recognize her," she said. "She's the one that murdered Hadley. She's trying to kill Tomek." Lennox set the photo array on the table in front of him.

He took a deep breath, his face wary. His eyes slid to the photo array. Then he picked it up, looked closer. He set the array back on the table and pointed to Jill's photo, pressed his thumb against the base of Jill's throat. "Terry," he said. "Who is she?"

"She works for the DA. She's a lawyer."

Pieter adjusted his arm in the sling, winced in pain. "Fuck," he said quietly.

"If we did a sting," she said.

"No sting."

"If I wanted to bust you for selling, it would've already come down."

"It's not going to happen," he said. "I won't sell to that bitch again."

"How can I convince you I want to catch Hadley's killer?"

"Why would I stick my neck out for Tomek's woman? I hated her. She made him think he was a smart guy, but all the time she was using him for drugs."

"What about Tomek?" she said.

He shook his head. "Tomek's not going to make it." He dropped his head to his chest. He didn't like saying it.

Lennox hoped with everything she had that Pieter was wrong about Tomek.

"It wouldn't work anyway," Pieter said. "Who'd believe us? You're not a cop anymore, and I'm a drug dealer. Terry works for the DA's office. How do we go up against her?"

No one would believe them. And even if they did, what did it prove? It was Pieter's word that the person buying drugs was Terry Purcell, the same person who Hadley called the night of her murder. Jill was the fucking prosecutor. How would Lennox take these flimsy connections and build a compelling case?

"There has to be a way we can trap her," Lennox said.

"We can't. We cut her off."

"Don't you see?" she said. "You're next."

He stood up. He looked smaller. The minute she stepped out the door, the locks snicked behind her.

CHAPTER 36

The next morning, Idzi was waiting on Lennox's porch swing reading Lennox's newspaper. Idzi had lost weight, her skin pinched up on her cheekbones, the lines deep around her mouth. Her designer jacket had an egg stain down the front.

"Thanks for not picking my locks," Lennox said. "Come in. I'll make coffee."

Idzi followed Lennox into the kitchen, eased herself into a kitchen chair. Gretchen licked Idzi's fingers and grinned that doggy grin of hers. "I heard you had a guard dog," Idzi said. She told Gretchen to sit, then pulled a dog biscuit from the crocodile bag. "Your friend, Jerry, was at the hospital this morning. Nice man. You have nice friends."

Lennox should despise this woman, but instead she felt strangely pleased that Idzi approved of her friends.

"Jerry told me I should go home and get some rest," Idzi said.

"That's a good idea."

"What I should do, I should find who's trying to kill

my boy." Idzi blew her nose, a great honk, into a dirty handkerchief. "Pieter tells me one of our customers, Terry Purcell, works for the DA. It was Terry that shot my boy."

Lennox sat down and leaned across the tiny table. "You know we're on the same team here."

Idzi nodded. "And you know Pieter will never agree to giving the cops proof that he is selling drugs."

"Even if I could promise immunity?"

Idzi shook her head and gave Lennox a touch of a smile, exhausted and knowing. "Immunity. They could promise it, he'll never get it."

"What if I sold drugs to Terry?"

"Pieter tells me you know this prosecutor?"

"Yes," Lennox said. "But I could go disguised." She felt ridiculous even suggesting it. She got up from the table and poured coffee for the two of them, brought the sugar bowl and a carton of milk over to the table. Each of them took turns spooning sugar, stirring milk.

"So we know this Terry disguises herself and buys drugs," Idzi said. "Why do you think she tried to kill Tomek?"

"Your son made the connection between Terry and Hadley. The way I've got it figured, Hadley went with Tomek when he made deliveries."

Idzi shook her head. "He wasn't supposed to bring her along. He wasn't even supposed to see her. When it comes to love, young people don't listen."

"Hadley recognized the woman posing as Terry Purcell," Lennox said. "Hadley blackmailed her. If it were known that this prosecutor posing as Terry is doing drugs, her career would be ruined."

"So, the best we can do is sell her drugs and ruin her career. How does this make Tomek safe?"

"You're right. I've got two people who IDed her for buying drugs." Two people who had no credibility in cop-land. "Everything else is circumstantial."

"Everything they have on my son is circumstantial," Idzi said. She was right. But which would the cops believe? A drug dealer or their boss?

They sat at the table drinking coffee, thinking. The coffee pot grumbled. A car drove down the street. Gretchen walked across the kitchen floor, her nails clicking on the vinyl, and stood at the back door.

Lennox let the dog out, then turned to Idzi, who sat with her fingertips pressed against her lips. The old woman said quietly, "If Terry is dead, no danger."

Lennox regretted every shitty decision she'd ever made, especially this one, the one to play it straight with the Jagodas. "I told you who Terry was because I trusted you not to do anything crazy."

The old woman fastened her dark eyes on Lennox. "Maybe you shouldn't have trusted me."

It was one way to resolve a case: have all the bad guys kill each other. Only who was really bad? "If you're willing to throw your life away like that, then you can help me with this sting," Lennox said. "If Terry's cornered she'll get violent. She's got to believe we're close to discovering who she is. That's why she made a second attempt to kill Tomek."

Idzi frowned at her coffee mug. "So I sell Terry drugs. And if the cops shoot her before she shoots me, then I'll be arrested for drug dealing."

Lennox opened her mouth to object, but Idzi waved dismissively. "Immunity. Okay, I'll do it."

240

At last they had a plan. "Does Terry ever contact you?"

"I typically route the deliveries." The old woman tilted her head with the resolute face of a warrior. Mess with her at your peril.

"Good. I've got some cop friends who trust me. I have to get them to sign on for this. I'll call you when I get it set up. We'll go from there."

CHAPTER 37

Lennox found Fish in the lobby of the Society Hotel in Chinatown. Built in the late 1800s, the hotel had been recently remodeled and made into a hip hostel-type place. It was just after lunch and a school of Japanese tourists, their bleached hair sleek with rain, giggled through the lobby, taking photos of each other on their phones. The tourists posed in front of the lobby's front window and posed in front of the stairway.

Fish sat on a wood bench across from the front desk and next to a potted palm, trying to look inconspicuous in gray and beige desert camouflage. Instead, he looked impossibly middle-aged and out of place.

Lennox sat herself next to him. "What are we doing here?" she whispered.

"OxyContin," he said in a low voice.

"Can I interest you in a big cocaine bust?"

"How big?"

She leaned closer to him, the potted palm nearly

brushing her eyebrow. "It's not the operation that's big," she said. "It's the user that's big."

"Oh, fuck," Fish said. "What have you done?"

"Jill Rykoff."

"What?" Fish said in a huge voice.

A couple of the tourists glanced at him in alarm.

"Goddamn, Cooper." His voice, a furious whisper. "You've finally lost it completely."

"Your prosecutor murdered Hadley Eberhart and shot Tomek Jagoda."

Fish stared at her like he couldn't believe Lennox had actually accused Rykoff of murder. "You're saying the prosecutor buys drugs from the Jagodas," he said. "Why would she do that? The Jagodas could blackmail her easy."

"She covers up her hair, wears men's clothes."

"But you recognize her because you're Dickless Tracy, queen of the detectives."

"I saw her buying drugs, and I've got her connected to the burner phone that Hadley Eberhart called the night of her murder. I figure Hadley was blackmailing Jill. And think about it, Fish, someone like Jill could've managed to get into one of the deputies' computers and engineered the early jail release for all those inmates. The only inmate that was shot was Jagoda, and he'd been out of jail less than two hours."

His heavy eyebrows hiked into his hairline. "Then why are you telling me and not your attorney?"

"I came to you because you're my go-to guy," Lennox said.

"No. You came to me because I'm in Vice. What you've got is a suspicion. Kline's a by-the-book attorney, and you won't tell him because your conclusions are based on a shitty amount of hard evidence."

"What we need is a sting," she said. "We'll catch her in the act. Do you think 2-K and Sarge would back us up?"

"Hell no," he said. "You realize busting her is going to raise a shit storm like we've never seen? The only reason I would be interested at all is finally getting Pieter Jagoda. With both her sons out of the picture, Old Lady Jagoda would have to retire."

"Not exactly," she said. She watched him play different scenarios in his head. Finally, he gave up and said, "Okay, Cooper, what dumb idea have you hatched this time?"

"Idzi Jagoda will make the call. She tells Jill she's got a shipment in at a great price. Big sale."

"Then what?" Fish said.

"Jill shows up at the site. You jump out, give her your spiel. She freaks and pulls a gun."

"Wait a minute. A gun? Really? That's your plan?" Fish said. "You want me to stand in the line of fire so you can bust some junkie that reminds you of our next DA."

"Not if you're running the investigation," she said. "You're in Vice. You provide Idzi with the drugs."

"Easy," he said. "Like checking out a library book. You know better than that, Cooper."

"Fine," she said. "I'll get my own drugs."

Fish shook his head. "You need more evidence before you're going to convince anyone in law enforcement that Rykoff is guilty of anything."

"So you're out of the deal?" Lennox could hardly believe she was saying it. "If it weren't for me, you'd still be sitting in a patrol car."

"You forget, I've saved your ass. More than once."

He shook his head. To give him credit, he looked as unhappy as she felt. Fish had always backed her up. Without him there was no sting. "What you're asking is a career-limiting move," he said. "For who? A drug dealer? Think about that when you're asking Sarge or 2-K to help you."

"I'm going to prove that I'm right about Rykoff."

No one was going to believe her or any of the Jagodas. But they would believe Kline.

CHAPTER 38

How to convince Kline that Jill was a murderer given what Lennox had for evidence? If Lennox couldn't get Fish to believe her—and Fish liked her—what chance did she have convincing Kline?

"What am I going to do?" she said out loud. Talking out loud to herself was becoming a thing. Thank God for Gretchen or she'd end up collecting cats.

Lennox held her head in her hands, her fingers clenched in her hair, hoping that maybe she could squeeze her brain into coming up with something. By late afternoon she had a plan. She made a series of calls, first to Idzi. "What kind of a shot are you?"

Damn good. And of course, Idzi had a gun.

"We're going to run a sting on Rykoff, only no drugs." Lennox told Idzi to bring the cell phone she used for dealing, her gun, and an extra clip. They would meet under the covered entrance at the Standard Insurance Building at 7:45. Then Lennox called Kline and told him that she'd solved the case. She set up a meeting for eight that night.

Lennox owned two ballistic vests. She needed one more. Her last call went to 2-K. She asked if could he drop off his ballistic vest after his shift.

"Are you in trouble?" He sounded worried. Good old 2-K. Why couldn't Fish be more like him? Lennox told him everything was good. She was close to ending the case. "That's just great," he said. He'd drop the vest off at six.

She spent the rest of the afternoon breaking down and servicing Old Ugly and the Glock. She checked both holsters, changed clothes, and stuffed her jacket pockets with spare magazines for both pistols.

After 2-K dropped off the vest, Lennox fed Gretchen, and let her outside. It had stopped raining, and the wind set Lennox's bird feeder swinging back and forth from the garage rafter.

She packed the three vests in a large sports bag, holstered the guns, and rubbed Gretchen's chin. If anything happened, Ham would know to rescue the dog. Lennox shrugged into her jacket and left.

She parked eight blocks away from Kline's office on the offhand chance Jill would spot the Bronco. The wind had turned colder, wetter. She only passed a handful of pedestrians wrapped in scarves, walking fast to get wherever they were going. Lennox hauled the sports bag on a shoulder strap, Old Ugly under her jacket, and the Glock in her ankle holster.

Idzi was waiting for her in front of Kline's office building. The old woman looked better: she'd washed her hair. Her face was less papery and lined.

Lennox tapped the glass door and motioned to Phil, the security guy, to let them in. Once Phil had found out

Lennox was a PI, he'd treated her like a rock star. He unlocked the door.

"You got evidence in that bag?" His tone was friendly and curious. She nodded.

"That's a lot of evidence. One of these days you got to tell me how it all works."

Lennox and Idzi walked past a janitor pushing an electric waxer across the lobby floor and took the elevators to the top floor of Bowersox, Kline and Hanson. The elevator opened onto the firm's waiting room. As always, it felt chilly. Without people, it was hushed, as if a film of snow had settled on the lobby furniture. There were no sounds of traffic from the street twenty-seven stories beneath them.

"Let's see what you got," Lennox said.

Idzi pulled a Makarov pistol and two extra magazines out of her bag and set them on the receptionist counter. If she would've dumped out a bandolier and strapped it across her old lady chest, Lennox wouldn't have been surprised.

"Good," Lennox said. "I'll give Kline the Glock."

They walked the carpeted hallway to Kline's office, knocked on his door, and entered without waiting for an answer.

Two desk lamps on either side of Kline's enormous desk lit the room. He looked up from his keyboard, the nightscape lit behind him: lights shining from the bridges, porch lights twinkling on the houses that clung to the sides of Mt. Tabor, and dozens of office lights in dozens of high rises lit by people like Kline, working late.

The starch had wilted from Kline's oxford shirt and lines etched deeply from his nose to his mouth. Lennox and Idzi took the chairs facing his desk. She hadn't laid eyes on him since the plea hearing. He glanced at her, then turned to Idzi.

"Mrs. Jagoda?" His voice gravelly. Lennox wondered if he was getting enough sleep.

"Ms. Cooper has found who tried to kill my Tomek," Idzi said.

"That's good." He turned to Lennox.

"It's Terry Purcell," Lennox said.

Kline looked pleased, then his expression turned bewildered. "Terry Purcell doesn't exist. It's some kind of alias."

"That's right," Lennox said.

"Terry is one of my customers." Idzi waited a moment to let that sink in. "Do you understand?"

Kline folded his hands on his desk. "I take it he's not one of your bakery customers."

Idzi's blackbird eyes glittered in the lamp light. She nodded slowly.

"I recognized him the night he made an attempt on Tomek's life," Lennox said. "And then again last night buying cocaine from Idzi's son, Pieter. You're not going to like what I tell you next, Gus."

Kline leaned forward in his chair and braced himself. "Let's hear it."

Lennox took a deep breath. Let it out. Now it was her turn to brace herself. "Jill Rykoff."

This time it wasn't just Kline's ears that turned red, it was his face, his neck. He looked like a heart attack. "You've got to be kidding me." He turned to Idzi and winced. "I'm sorry that my colleague has somehow persuaded you with this nonsense."

"We can prove it," Lennox said. "This minute. But you

have to know, if I prove to you that Jill's guilty, she'll go after you the way she went after Hadley and Tomek."

His mouth twisted into a half-smile. "Yeah. Sure."

"There's no going back, Gus," Lennox said.

"Don't worry about me."

But she did. Lennox believed she loved Kline, and she was putting him in harm's way. She sent out a prayer to Luck. Sometimes that worked.

She nodded to Idzi.

Idzi pulled her cellphone from her handbag and punched in a number. Put her finger to her lips and hit the speaker button. Kline and Lennox heard the phone ring. On the third ring, Rykoff answered the phone. "Idzi," she said. She'd pitched her voice to a lower register. "What's up?"

Lennox glanced at Kline. His eyes went very wide. Had he heard that low voice over cocktails? Making pillow talk? Lennox fisted her hands to keep steady, to focus on the end game.

"I got a new shipment of high-grade blow for a very good price," Idzi said. "I thought of you."

Rykoff hesitated. "I just bought some."

Kline leaned in towards the phone.

"How good a price?" Rykoff finally said.

"It's Jill," Kline said. He slapped his hand over his mouth.

There was a beat, then the line went dead.

"This is the way it had to be," Lennox said.

Idzi nodded in agreement.

Kline threw himself back in his chair, swiped his hand across his mouth, blinked. Lennox would like to think that he hated to see a prosecutor accused of murder. But the guy looked stricken, like his whole reality underwent a seismic shift. It was more than a corrupt colleague: she'd seen that same look in the mirror when her romantic life had hit the wall.

Kline looked wearily at Lennox. Whatever he was feeling, right now she had to convince him that Jill was not just a user, but a murderer. And then she had to get him to sign on to her plan. She lined out her case, beginning with the call Hadley made to Terry Purcell. Lennox believed that Hadley had recognized Jill when she tagged along with Tomek as he made his drug deliveries. When Hadley called Terry aka Jill that night, it was Jill's intention to murder her. That's why she brought the drug packet with Tomek's fingerprint on it to plant at the murder site. Jill probably brought her .22, the same one that she shot Tomek with, but when she saw what kind of shape Hadley was in, she drowned her. The gloves came from Jeff's garage. Jill pulled them on, drowned Hadley, then planted the gloves in a dumpster near Tomek's house."

"How much of this can you prove?"

"We just have proof that Jill is masquerading as Terry Purcell."

"Yes," Kline said. "But what hard evidence do you have?"

"Tomek was indicted on a phone call, a fingerprint and the fact that he was Hadley's boyfriend. I've been trying to tell you that Hadley's murder and Tomek's shooting are connected. Someone in law enforcement released those prisoners from jail. Someone shot Tomek an hour after he was released."

Lennox tried to get a read on Kline. She glanced at Idzi, who was watching him as well. He looked like he'd bought the story most of the way.

"But you realize this isn't enough to take to a judge," he said.

"It's enough to raise questions about her competency. Now that you know about her, she'll try to kill you."

"So, I'll—" He paused, looking even more miserable. "Never mind."

Idzi cleared her throat. "Lennox figures it'll go down in the parking garage. The sooner she takes care of you, the better. She's not worried about me. I'm old. And no judge would listen to me."

"Say Jill's at her office. She'd have to drive home and get her weapon. That's twenty minutes minimum." Lennox said. "Ten minutes if she was already home."

"Weapon," Kline said heavily.

Lennox bent down and unholstered her Glock, then laid it on his desk. "Do you know how to use one of these?" she said.

"You want me to shoot the assistant DA?" he said.

"I want you to be able to defend yourself. Your accusation that Jill is dirty would carry some weight," Lennox said. "With you out of the way, it's my word against the prosecuting attorney. How far do you think I'd get with that? Show me that you know how to handle the gun."

"I'm a defense attorney, for chrissake," he muttered. He ejected the clip, racked the gun, checked the chamber, then inserted the clip and racked the gun again.

Okay then. Lennox reached into her bag and pulled out two bulletproof vests. Told Idzi and Kline to put them on.

Kline hesitated and looked miserable all over again.

"Put it on," Idzi said. And struggled into hers. It hung nearly to her thighs.

"What level are you parked on?" Lennox said to Kline.

"P-3."

Lennox walked over to the light switch and turned on the overhead lights. Both Kline and Idzi looked pale and worried.

"We'll take the elevators to your lobby. The stairs to your parking level."

He nodded.

"She'll drive past your office, see your lights, and know you're working late. Turn the lights off at 8:45. Wait until nine, then take the parking elevator. Have the gun racked, and hold it next to your leg. If the elevator isn't functioning, stay put. Do not take the stairwell. Do not exit the elevator until you hear my voice. Do you understand?"

He looked like a big lump of misery.

"Are you sure you're up for this?" Lennox said. She'd never seen so much emotion on his face—disbelief, fear, disappointment. She felt sorry for him. Sorry for herself.

"We got to go," Idzi said.

CHAPTER 39

"You realize we need to have Kline witness whatever goes down," Lennox said in the elevator.

Idzi nodded. In her ballistics vest, the old lady looked like a little turtle with a shell too big for her.

"Still. We have to defend ourselves," Lennox said.

Idzi half-smiled. "I get it."

They left the lobby and crossed the street to the parking garage.

They quietly took the three flights of stairs to P-3. Lennox stopped a couple times to wait for Idzi, but the old lady waved away Lennox's concern. Idzi had the person responsible for Tomek's suffering in her sights.

Lennox thumbed off the safety on Old Ugly, and Idzi racked her pistol. The sound filled the stairwell. They looked at each other and waited for the sound of footsteps, for a gunshot. The only sound was traffic splashing through the puddled street three floors below. They stood to the side of the stair opening and as far back as possible. Lennox pointed Ugly up and against her face and edged around the corner until she could see the third floor of the parking garage. Her eyes and ears strained for any movement, any sound. The elevator was catty corner to the stairwell; Kline's BMW was parked two spaces from the elevator in an area marked "reserved." Two Priuses were parked against the half wall, a Volkswagen next to Kline's BMW, and a Subaru parked by a support pillar facing the stairwell.

"Head to the Subaru, then get behind the support pillar. I'll cover you," she whispered to Idzi. The old lady moved stiffly but rapidly. Once Idzi stood safely behind the cement pillar on the far side of the Subaru, Lennox edged along the garage wall, ducking behind the parked cars until she stood behind the pillar on the far side of the garage from Idzi.

8:35. Fog seeped over the concrete half-walls. The garage was cold and smelled of cement dust. Lennox kept her eyes peeled, her teeth clenched to keep them from chattering. She checked her sight lines, figuring Jill would hide behind the support pillar closest to the elevator, an unobstructed shot for Lennox. Alternatively, Jill could take cover behind the VW. Lennox would have to step from behind cover, but she could manage, with luck.

Lennox was trembling from the cold, her fingers growing stiff. She changed Ugly from hand to hand, edging around the pillar, taking aim from one hiding spot, then the next. Watching the stairwell, the elevator. Listening for any sound. Time crawled. She quick glanced at her watch. 8:50.

Jill entered the garage slowly from the stairwell, silent as a cat, wearing the same knit cap she wore when she was posing as Terry. Jill looked over the parked cars, pulled a .22 rifle from her open coat, and racked the bolt action. Then Jill crouched on the floor and looked under the Priuses.

Lennox hid behind the column, held her breath. Hoped

that Idzi saw Jill in time to move out of Jill's sight-line. Lennox was freezing; she was sweating.

Jill made her way to the VW, crouched behind it and took aim at the elevator doors. Then she stood up and trotted to the cement pillar closest to the elevator, took aim once more at the elevator door, then remained still.

Five minutes crawled by. Jill remained silent and hidden.

Another five minutes passed. The elevator hydraulics whirred. Show time.

The elevator door opened.

"Watch out!" Lennox shouted to Kline.

Jill turned and fired at Lennox. The explosion of the .22 amplified off the cement floor and ceiling. The bullet hit the corner of the cement support. Lennox was grazed by something sharp. Blood trickled down her face. The VW's car alarm went off. Gunpowder smoke mixed with the dust.

The elevator door closed, then opened again. Lennox waited until Jill lifted from cover, then took her shot. The bullet ricocheted off one of the Priuses.

Jill crouched and pulled the bolt action, then stood. Then Idzi came out from behind the Subaru and shot. Jill fell to the floor.

More car alarms, sirens screaming.

Kline came out of the elevator holding the Glock in both hands. "Cooper," he yelled. "Where are you?"

Lennox told him to hold back. She kept her gun trained on Jill and walked closer. Jill was curled in a fetal position, gasping in pain. Lennox kicked the rifle out of reach.

It was over. They heard the sirens a block away.

Idzi and Kline walked over to Jill. Blood seeped from her wound and onto the cement floor. A look of intense satisfaction played across Idzi's face when she saw that Jill was gut shot. Kline looked from Jill's crumpled body to Idzi, then to Lennox. Everything Lennox had been telling him was sinking in as he watched Jill gasp with pain. She had killed Hadley, shot Tomek, and had come here tonight to kill him.

"Tell me," he said.

"Jill shot at me. Idzi shot Jill."

"Is there anything we should do for her?" he said. Maybe it was the cold or maybe it was nerves that made him shiver.

"The first responders will be here any minute," Lennox said.

"We're telling them it was self-defense," he told Idzi. "They'll hold you for questioning. Don't say a word until I get there."

The noise from the sirens was deafening when the cops pulled into the garage. They laid their guns down on the floor and had their hands up when the cops reached them. One of the cops told Lennox she was bleeding.

There were a whole lot of questions. The ambulance hauled Jill away. A fireman cleaned and bandaged Lennox's cheekbone. Despite Kline's protestations, Idzi was cuffed and taken into custody. Kline jumped into his car to follow them. Lennox went home.

She turned the thermostat up, built a fire in the fireplace, poured herself a triple shot of Kline's scotch, petted the dog, but still, she couldn't get warm. It was like that for the rest of the night.

CHAPTER 40

Kline slid the bonus check across his large desk. It was enough to pay three months rent on Lennox's office, or to pay her expenses sans office while she hustled for more work.

He unlocked a desk drawer and pushed her Glock across the desk.

"Can't we talk about this?" she said.

"What part of this do you want to discuss?" he circled his hand around the check and the gun.

"I apologize for telling Tomek about the plea."

"Well, you were right about him. About Rykoff, too. I guess you figure so long as you end up right in the end…" His voice trailed off. Kline made right sound worse than wrong.

"I heard from Idzi. Tomek's getting released from Providence at the end of the week."

He nodded. "I suppose now that he's recovered, he'll go on to teaching kindergarten and give up his life of crime."

"Hard to know." But Lennox had a good guess. Tomek

would continue to read about wizards and dragons, feed his birds, and do whatever his mother told him to do. Maybe the old woman would teach him how to work in the bakery.

Lennox studied Kline from across the vast distance that spanned his desk. His gray eyes were opaque. Did he mourn Jill's death? Did he kick himself for liking Jill too much, for misjudging her? Lennox wanted to tell him how she'd come to realize that she cared for him. Maybe it was wrong to believe that they could be anything more than co-workers. She would settle for co-workers.

"So, we're done?" she said.

She didn't have to ask. She knew done when she saw it. She squared her shoulders. "Just so you know, I'm not giving Gretchen back."

"If anything happens to her—" Kline closed his eyes, then opened them. "I don't know what I'll do."

He swiveled his chair so that he faced the glass wall behind him. The gold seals on all his diplomas shone dull in the late afternoon light. He was done with her.

Mrs. Tamer had been right. The king of swords, the ten of pentacles reversed. "He's not the one," she'd said. That's how desperate Lennox had become, going back to a psychic to find out about her love life. As P.T. Barnum had said, there's one born every minute.

Lennox stood up and looked at the back of his chair. "It was a great privilege having worked for you," she said. Not strictly true. It took two martinis to make him even human, but she'd miss him. His sarcasm, his intelligence, the way he smelled, this freezing office. Walking out of Kline's office broke her heart.

• • •

Lennox opened the Shanty's front door. The Shanty crew had done their best with sorry-looking brown and orange themed Thanksgiving decorations. Cardboard turkeys crowned with pilgrims' hats. There was nothing worse than facing the holidays, nearly forty and still single with only a withered, hundred-pound, cranky mother for a family.

Fish popped off his stool and nudged her with his elbow. That was about as physical as it got with Fish. "Why the long face?"

"It's a long story."

"You going to forgive me, Cooper?" he said. His mouth straight and serious. He looked truly sorry.

Lennox wanted to see him squirm a little more, but truth be told, any cop in their right mind wouldn't have gone after a prosecutor based on what she had offered as a case. Lennox had taken a big chance going after Jill. Lennox was reckless, she knew that about herself.

A couple of cops she recognized turned from the bar as she walked by. "It's Dirty Harriette," one of them said. The other one chuckled.

The back room smelled like pepperoni and Jerry's scotch.

"Congrats, Sherlock," Jerry said.

"I always get my man," she said. It wasn't funny on a couple of levels. No one else thought it was funny, either. She reached in her bag and passed Ham five twenties, then ordered a drink from Katy, the cocktailer.

Ham unwrapped a new deck of cards and discarded the jokers. They all sat around the stained table, looking at each other, tidying stacks of chips, sipping off drinks.

"Who are we waiting for?" Fish said.

"New guy," Ham said. "He said he's on his way."

"Goody," Lennox said. "Fresh meat."

The door opened and Katy walked into the room with a tray full of drinks. Trailing behind her was August Kline in jeans and a brown crew neck sweater.

Ham motioned Kline to the chair next to him. "You know Coop, of course," Ham said.

Of course.

Ham finished introducing Kline to the rest of the guys. Lennox knew she was staring pop-eyed and open-mouthed at Kline. Fresh meat, indeed.

"You play poker?" she said.

"I bought my first car with poker money," Kline said.

Of course. The bill of sale was probably stamped with a gold seal of approval and expensively framed on his office wall. You had to love this guy.

Ham announced the game: seven-card stud hi/low eight or better. Lennox settled in her chair and waited for the peek.

My gratitude to Liz, agent and lovely friend. To the folks at Diversion Books. To Jim Frey, brilliant storyteller, teacher and friend. To Susan Whitcher for your friendship, brainstorming, and critique. Barbara Davis Kroon: ditto. To Caroline Kurtz and Raina Croff. To Martha Miller, Martha Ragland, Susan Clayton Goldner, Susan Kelly, and all the wise, witty, and generous folks at FWOF.

And to Michael, at the heart of everything I write.

Lily Gardner lives in Portland with her husband, two corgis, and several thousand books. *A Bitch Called Hope* was her first Lennox Cooper mystery, followed by *Betting Blind*. *All In* is the third in the series.

Visit her web site (**www.lilygardner.net**), Facebook page (**www.facebook.com/authorLilyGardner**) or email her at **lilygardnermystery@gmail.com**.

Thank you for reading *All In*. If you enjoyed this book, please consider leaving a review on Amazon and Goodreads. Reviews are gold to authors!

CPSIA information can be obtained
at www.ICGtesting.com
Printed in the USA
BVOW09s1438260418
514484BV00001B/2/P